MARJORIE AT SEACOTE

CAROLYN WELLS

1st WORLD
LIBRARY
Literary Society

Marjorie at Seacote

Carolyn Wells

© 1st World Library, 2006
PO Box 2211
Fairfield, IA 52556
www.1stworldlibrary.com
First Edition

LCCN: 2006937736

Softcover ISBN: 978-1-4218-3317-0
Hardcover ISBN: 978-1-4218-3217-3
eBook ISBN: 978-1-4218-3417-7

Purchase *"Marjorie at Seacote"*
as a traditional bound book at:
www.1stWorldLibrary.com/purchase.asp?ISBN=978-1-4218-3317-0

1ˢᵗ World Library Literary Society

Giving Back to the World

"If you want to work on the core problem, it's early school literacy."

- James Barksdale, former CEO of Netscape

"No skill is more crucial to the future of a child, or to a democratic and prosperous society, than literacy."

- Los Angeles Times

Literacy... means far more than learning how to read and write... The aim is to transmit... knowledge and promote social participation."

- UNESCO

"Literacy is not a luxury, it is a right and a responsibility. If our world is to meet the challenges of the twenty-first century we must harness the energy and creativity of all our citizens."

- President Bill Clinton

"Parents should be encouraged to read to their children, and teachers should be equipped with all available techniques for teaching literacy, so the varying needs and capacities of individual kids can be taken into account."

- Hugh Mackay

CONTENTS

CHAPTER I

KITTY'S DINNER

"Kitty-Cat Kitty is going away,
Going to Grandma's, all summer to stay.
And so all the Maynards will weep and will bawl,
Till Kitty-Cat Kitty comes home in the fall."

This affecting ditty was being sung with great gusto by King
and Marjorie, while Kitty, her mood divided between smiles
and tears, was quietly appreciative.

The very next day, Kitty was to start for Morristown, to spend
the summer with Grandma Sherwood, and to-night the
"Farewell Feast" was to be celebrated.

Every year one of the Maynard children spent the summer
months with their grandmother, and this year it was Kitty's
turn. The visit was always a pleasant one, and greatly enjoyed
by the small visitor, but there was always a wrench at parting,
for the Maynard family were affectionate and deeply devoted
to one another.

The night before the departure was always celebrated by a
festival of farewell, and at this feast tokens were presented, and
speeches made, and songs sung, all of which went far to dispel
sad or gloomy feelings.

The Maynards were fond of singing. They were willing to sing "ready-made" songs, and often did, but they liked better to make up songs of their own, sometimes using familiar tunes and sometimes inventing an air as they went along. Even if not quite in keeping with the rules for classic music, these airs were pleasing in their own ears, and that was all that was necessary.

So, when King and Midget composed the touching lines which head this chapter and sang them to the tune of "The Campbells are Coming," they were so pleased that they repeated them many times.

This served to pass pleasantly the half-hour that must yet elapse before dinner would be announced.

"Well, Kit," remarked Kingdon, in a breathing pause between songs, "we'll miss you lots, o' course, but you'll have a gay old time at Grandma's. That Molly Moss is a whole team in herself."

"She's heaps of fun, Kitsie," said Marjorie, "but she's chock-a-block full of mischief. But you won't tumble head over heels into all her mischiefs, like I did! 'Member how I sprained my ankle, sliding down the barn roof with her?"

"No, of course I wouldn't do anything like that," agreed the sedate Kitty. "But we'll have lots of fun with that tree-house; I'm going to sit up there and read, on pleasant days."

"H'm,—lucky,—you know what, King!"

"H'm,—yes! Keep still, Mops. You'll give it away."

"Oh, a secret about a present," cried Kitty; "something for the tree-house, I know!"

"Maybe 'tis, and maybe 'tain't," answered King, with a mysterious wink at Marjorie.

"Me buyed present for Kitty," said Rosamond, smiling sweetly;

"gold an' blue,—oh, a bootiful present."

"Hush, hush, Rosy Posy, you mustn't tell," said her brother. "Presents are always surprises. Hey, girls, here's Father!"

Mr. Maynard's appearance was usually a signal for a grand rush, followed by a series of bear hugs and a general scramble, but to-night, owing to festive attire, the Maynard quartette were a little more demure.

"Look out for my hair-ribbons, King!" cried Midget, for without such warning, hair-ribbons usually felt first the effects of the good-natured scrimmage.

And then Mrs. Maynard appeared, her pretty rose-colored gown of soft silk trailing behind her on the floor.

"What a dandy mother!" exclaimed King; "all dressed up, and a flower in her hair!"

This line sounded singable to Marjorie, so she tuned up:

"All dressed up, and a flower in her hair,
To give her a hug, I wouldn't dare;
For she would feel pretty bad, I think,
If anything happened to that there pink!"

Then King added a refrain, and in a moment they had all joined hands and were dancing round Mrs. Maynard and singing:

"Hooray, hooray, for our mother fair!
Hooray, hooray, for the flower in her hair!
All over the hills and far away,
There's no one so sweet as Mothery May!"

Being accustomed to boisterous adulation from her children, Mrs. Maynard bore her honors gracefully, and then they all went out to dinner.

As Maiden of Honor, Kitty was escorted by her father; next came Mrs. Maynard and Kingdon, and then Marjorie and Rosy Posy. The table had extra decorations of flowers and pink-shaded candles, and at Kitty's place was a fascinating looking lot of tissue-papered and ribbon-tied parcels.

"Isn't it funny," said sedate and philosophical Kitty, "I love to go to Grandma's, and yet I hate to leave you all, and yet, I can't do one without doing the other!"

"'Tis strange, indeed, Kit!" agreed her father; "as Mr. Shakespeare says, 'Yet every sweet with sour is tempered still.' Life is like lemonade, sour and sweet both."

"It's good enough," said Kitty, contentedly, looking at her array of bundles. "I guess I'll open these now."

"That's what they're there for," said Mrs. Maynard, so Kitty excitedly began to untie the ribbons.

"I'll go slowly," she said, pulling gently at a ribbon bow, "then they'll last longer."

"Now, isn't that just like you, Kit!" exclaimed Marjorie. "I'd snatch the papers off so fast you couldn't see me jerk."

"I know you would," said Kitty, simply.

The sisters were very unlike, for Midget's ways were impulsive and impatient, while Kitty was slow and careful. But finally the papers came off, and revealed the lovely gifts.

Mrs. Maynard had made a pretty silk workbag, which could be spread out, or gathered up close on its ribbon. When outspread, it showed a store of needles and thread, of buttons, hooks, tapes,—everything a little girl could need to keep her clothes in order.

"Oh, Mother, it's *perfect*!" cried Kitty, ecstatically. "I *love* those

Carolyn Wells

cunning little pockets, with all *sewy* things in them! And a darling silver thimble! And a silver tape measure, and a silver-topped emery! Oh, I do believe I'll sew *all* the time this summer!"

"Pooh, *I* wouldn't!" said Marjorie. "The things *are* lovely, but I'd rather play than sew."

"Sewing *is* play, I think," and Kitty fingered over her treasures lovingly. "Grandma will help me with my patterns, and I'm going to piece a silk teachest quilt. Oh, Mother, it will be *such* fun!"

"Call *that* fun!" and Marjorie looked disdainfully at her sister. "Fun is racing around and playing tag, and cutting up jinks generally!"

"For you it is," Kitty agreed, amiably, "but not for me. I like what I like."

"That's good philosophy, Kitty," said her father. "Stick to it always. Like what you like, and don't be bothered by other people's comments or opinions. Now, what's in that smallish, flattish, whitish parcel?"

The parcel in question proved to be a watch, a dear little gold watch. Kitty had never owned one before, and it almost took her breath away.

"Mine?" she exclaimed, in wonder. "All mine?"

"Yes, every bit yours," said Mr. Maynard, smiling at her. "Every wheel and spring, every one of its three hands, every one of its twelve hours are all, all yours. Do you like it?"

"Like it! I can't think of any words to tell you how much I like it."

"I'll think of some for you," said the accommodating Marjorie.

"You could say it's the grandest, gloriousest, gorgeousest, magnificentest present you ever had!"

"Yes, I could say that," Kitty agreed, "but I never should have thought of it. I 'most always say a thing is lovely. Now, what in the world is this?"

"This" proved to be a well-stocked portfolio, the gift of King. There were notepaper and envelopes and a pen and pencils and stamps and everything to write letters with.

"I picked out all the things myself," King explained, "because it's nicer that way than the ready furnished ones. Do you like it, Kit?"

"Yes, indeedy! And I shall write my first letter to you, because you gave it to me."

"Oh, Kitty-Cat Kit, a letter she writ,
And sent it away, to her brother one day,"

chanted Marjorie, and, as was their custom, they all sang the song after her, some several times over.

"Now for mine," Midget said, as Kitty slowly untied the next parcel. It was two volumes of Fairy Tales, which literature was Kitty's favorite reading.

"Oh, lovely!" she exclaimed. "On summer afternoons you can think of me, sitting out in the tree-house reading these. I shall pretend I'm a Fairy Princess. These are beautiful stories, I can see that already."

Kitty's quick eye had caught an interesting page, and forgetting all else, she became absorbed in the book at once. In a moment, the page was turned, and Kitty read on and on, oblivious to time or place.

"Hi, there , Kitsie! Come out o' that!" cried King. "You can read all summer,—*now* you must associate with your family."

"I didn't mean to," said Kitty, shutting the book quickly, and looking round apologetically; "but it's all about a fairy godmother, and a lovely princess lady,—oh, Mopsy, it's *fine!*"

A pair of little blue enamelled pins was Rosamond's present, and Kitty pinned them on her shoulders at once, to see how they looked. All pronounced the effect excellent, and Rosy Posy clapped her little fat hands in glee.

"Mine's the prettiest present!" she said. "Mine's the booflest!"

"Yes, Babykins," said Kitty, "yours is the booflest,—but they're all lovely."

The Farewell Feast included all of Kitty's favorite dishes, and as most of them were also favorites with the other children, it was satisfactory all round.

"You must write to us often, Kit," said King; "I gave you those writing things so you'd be sure to."

"Yes, I will; but I don't know yet where you're all going to be."

"I don't know yet myself," said Mr. Maynard, "but it will be somewhere near the sea, if possible. Will you like the seashore, Kiddies,—you that are going?"

"I shall," said Marjorie, promptly. "I'll *love* it. May we go bathing every day? And can I have a bathing suit,—red, trimmed with white?"

"I 'spect you can," said her mother, smiling at her. "What color do you want, King?"

"Oh, I think dark blue would suit my manly beauty! What are you going to have, Father?"

"I think dark blue will be our choice, my boy. It swims better than anything else. But first we must find a roof to cover our heads. I've about decided on one,—if I can get it. It's a bungalow."

"What's a bungalow?" asked Marjorie. "I never heard of such a thing."

"Ho, ho! Never heard of a bungalow!" said King. "Why, a bungalow is a,—is a,—"

"Well, is a what?" asked Midget, impatiently.

"Why, it's a bungalow! That's what it is."

"Fine definition, King!" said his father. "But since you undertook to do so, see if you can't give its meaning better than that. What *is* a bungalow?"

"Well, let me see. It's a house,—I guess it's a low, one-storied house, and that's why they call it bungalow. Is that it?"

"You're right about the one story; the rest is, I think, your own invention. Originally, the bungalow was the sort of a house they have in India, a one-storied affair, with a thatched roof, and verandas all round it. But the ones they build now, in this country, are often much more elaborate than that. Sometimes they have one story, sometimes more. The one I'm trying to get for the summer is at Seacote, and it's what they call a story and a half. That is, it has an upper floor, but the rooms are under a slanting roof, and have dormer windows."

"Sounds good to me," said King. "Do you think you'll catch it, Dad?"

"I hope so. Some other person has the refusal of it, but he's doubtful about taking it. So it may yet fall to our lot."

"I hope so!" cried Marjorie. "At the seashore for a whole

summer! My! what fun! Can we dig in the sand?"

"Well, rather, my child! That's what the sand is there for. Kitty, you were at the seashore last summer. Did you dig in the sand?"

"Yes, every day; and it was lovely. But this year I'm glad I'm going to Grandma's. It's more restful."

They all laughed at Kitty's desire for rest, and Marjorie said:

"*I* didn't have such a restful time at Grandma's. Except when I sprained my ankle,—I rested enough then! But you won't do anything like that, Kit!"

"I hope not, I'm sure. Nor I won't fall down the well, either!"

"Oh, we didn't *fall* down the well. We just *went* down, to get cooled off."

"Well, I'm not going to try it. I shall sit in the tree-house and read every afternoon, and sew with Grandma in the mornings."

"Kit, you're a dormouse," said Kingdon; "I believe you'd like to sleep half the year."

"'Deed I wouldn't. Just because I don't like rambunctious play doesn't mean I want to sleep all the time! Does it, Father?"

"Not a bit of it. But you children must 'like what you like' and not comment on others' 'likes.' See?"

"Yes, sir," said King, understanding the kindly rebuke. "Hullo, Kit, here's one of your best 'likes'! Here's pink ice-cream coming!"

This was indeed one of Kitty's dearest "likes," and as none of the Maynards disliked it, it rapidly disappeared.

"Now, we'll have an entertainment," said King as, after dinner, they all went back to the pleasant living-room. "As Kitty is the chief pebble on the beach this evening, she shall choose what sort of an entertainment. Games, or what?"

"No, just a real entertainment," said Kitty; "a programme one, you know. Each one must sing a song or speak a piece, or something like that. *I'll* be the audience, and you can all be performers."

"All right," said King; "I'll be master of ceremonies. I'll make up the programme as I go along. Ladies and gentlemen, our first number will be a speech by the Honorable Edward Maynard. Mr. Maynard will please step forward."

Mr. Maynard stepped. Assuming a pompous air, he made a low bow, first to Kitty, and then to the others.

"My dear friends," he said, "we are gathered here together this evening to extend our farewells and our hearty good wishes to the lady about to leave us. Sister, thou art mild and lovely, and we hate to see thee go; but the best of friends must sever, and you'll soon come back, you know. Listen now to our advices. Kitty, dear, for pity's sake, do not tumble in the river,—do not tumble in the lake. Many more things I could tell you as I talk in lovely rhyme, but I think it is my duty to let others share the time."

Mr. Maynard sat down amid great applause, and Kitty said, earnestly, "You are a lovely poet, Father. I wish you'd give up your other business, and just write books of poetry."

"I'm afraid, Kitsie, we wouldn't have enough money for pink ice-cream in that case," said Mr. Maynard, laughing.

"The next performeress will be Mrs. Maynard," announced the master of ceremonies.

Mother Maynard rose, smiling, and with all the airs and graces of a prima donna, went to the piano. Striking a few preliminary chords, she began to sing:

"Good-bye, Kitty; good-bye, Kitty; good-bye, Kitty,
You're going to leave us now.
Merrily we say good-bye,
Say good-bye, say good-bye;
Merrily we say good-bye
To sister Kitty-Kit."

This had a pleasant jingle, and was repeated by the whole assembly with fine effect and a large volume of noise.

"Miss Marjorie Maynard will now favor us," was the next announcement.

"This is a poem I made up myself," said Midget, modestly, "and I think it's very nice:

"When Kitty goes to Grandma's
I hope she will be good;
And be a lady-girl and do
Exactly as she should.
'Cause when *I go* to Grandma's,
I act exceeding bad;
I track up 'Liza's nice clean floor,
And make her hopping mad!"

Marjorie's poem was applauded with cheers, as they all recognized its inherent truth.

"We next come to Miss Rosamond Maynard," King went on, "but as she has fallen asleep, I will ask that the audience kindly excuse her."

The audience kindly did so, and as it was getting near everybody's bedtime,—at least, for children,—the whole quartette was started bedward, and went away singing:

"Good-bye, Kitty, you're going to leave us now"—

CHAPTER II

TOM, DICK, AND HARRY

"Jumping Grasshoppers! What a dandy house!"

The Maynards' motor swung into the driveway of a large and pleasant looking place, whose lawn showed some sand spots here and there, and whose trees were tall pines, but whose whole effect was delightfully breezy and seashorey.

"Oh, grandiferous!" cried Marjorie, echoing her brother's enthusiastic tones, and standing up in the car, better to see their new home.

Seacote, the place chosen by Mr. Maynard for his family's summering, was on the southern shore of Long Island, not very far from Rockaway Beach. It was a sort of park or reservation in which building was under certain restrictions, and so it was made up of pleasant homes filled with pleasant people.

Fortunately, Mr. Maynard had been able to rent the bungalow he wanted, and it was this picturesque domicile that so roused King's admiration.

The house was long and low, and surrounded by verandas, some of which were screened by vines, and others shaded by striped awnings.

But what most delighted the children was the fact that the ocean rolled its crested breakers up to their very door. Not literally to the door, for the road ran between the sea and the house, and a boardwalk was between the road and the sea. But not fifty feet from their front windows the shining waves were even now dashing madly toward them as if in tumultuous welcome.

The servants were already installed, and the open doors seemed to invite the family to come in and make themselves at home.

"Let's go straight bang through the whole house," said King, "and then outdoors afterward."

"All right," agreed Marjorie, and in their usual impetuous fashion, the two raced through the house from attic to cellar, though there really wasn't any attic, except a sort of low-ceiled loft. However, they climbed up into this, and then down through the various bedrooms on the second floor, and back to the first floor, which contained the large living-room, a spacious hall, and the dining-room and kitchen.

"It's all right," said King, nodding his head in approval. "Now outside, Midget."

Outside they flew, and took stock of their surroundings. Almost an acre of ground was theirs, and though as yet empty of special interest, King could see its possibilities.

"Room for a tennis court," he said; "then I guess we'll have a big swing, and a hammock, and a tent, and—"

"And a merry-go-round," supplemented Mr. Maynard, overhearing King's plans.

"No, not that, Father," said Marjorie, "but we *can* have swings and things, can't we?"

"I 'spect so, Mopsy. But with the ocean and the beach, I doubt if you'll stay in this yard much."

"Oh, that's so; I forgot the ocean! Come on, Father, let's go and look at it."

So the three went down to the beach, and Marjorie, who hadn't been to the seashore since she was a small child, plumped herself down on the sand, and just gazed out at the tumbling waves.

"I don't care for the swings and things," she said. "I just want to stay here all the time, and dig and dig and dig."

As she spoke she was digging her heels into the fine white sand, and poking her hands in, and burying her arms up to her dimpled elbows.

"Oh, Father, isn't it gee-lorious! Sit down, won't you, and let us bury you in sand, all but your nose!"

"Not now," said Mr. Maynard, laughing. "Some day you may, when I'm in a bathing suit. But I don't care for pockets full of sand. Now, I'm going back to home and Mother. You two may stay down here till luncheon time if you like."

Mr. Maynard went back to the house, and King and Marjorie continued their explorations. The beach was flat and smooth, and its white sand was full of shells, and here and there a few bits of seaweed, and farther on some driftwood, and in the distance a pier, built out far into the ocean.

"Did you ever *see* such a place?" cried Marjorie, in sheer delight.

"Well, I was at the seashore last year," said King, "while you were at Grandma's."

"But it wasn't as nice as this, was it? Say it wasn't!"

"No; the sand was browner. This is the nicest sand I ever saw. Say, Mops, let's build a fire."

"What for? It isn't cold."

"No, but you always build fires on the beach. It's lots of fun. And we'll roast potatoes in it."

"All right. How do we begin?"

"Well, we gather a lot of wood first. Come on."

Marjorie came on, and they worked with a will, gathering armfuls of wood and piling it up near the spot they had selected for their fire.

"That's enough," said Marjorie, for her arms ached as she laid down her last contribution to their collection.

"You'll find it isn't much when it gets to burning. But never mind, it will make a start. I'll skin up to the house and get matches and potatoes."

"I'll go with you, 'cause I think we'd better ask Father about making this fire. It might do some harm."

"Fiddlesticks! We made a fire 'most every day last summer."

And, owing to King's knowledge and experience regarding beach fires, his father told him he might build one, and to be properly careful about not setting fire to themselves.

Then they procured potatoes and apples from the kitchen, and raced back to the beach.

"Why, where's our wood?" cried Marjorie.

Not a stick or a chip remained of their carefully gathered wood pile.

"Some one has stolen it!" said King.

"No, there's nobody around, except those people over there, and they're grown-ups. It must have been washed away by a wave."

"Pooh, the waves aren't coming up near as far as this."

"Well, there might have been a big one."

"No, it wasn't a wave. That wood was stolen, Mops!"

"But who could have done it? Those grown-up people wouldn't. You can see from their looks they wouldn't. They're reading aloud. And in the other direction, there are only some fishermen,—they wouldn't take it."

"Well, somebody did. Look, here are lots of footprints, and I don't believe they're all ours."

Sure enough, on the smooth white sand they could see many footprints, imprinted all over each other, as if scurrying feet had trodden all around their precious wood pile.

"Oh, King, you're just like a detective!" cried Marjorie, in admiration. "But it's so! These aren't our footprints!"

She fitted her spring-heeled tan shoes into the prints, and proved at once that they were not hers. Nor did King's shoes fit exactly, though they came nearer to it than Marjorie's.

"Yes, sir; some fellows came along and stole that wood. Here are two or three quite different prints."

"Well, where do they lead to?" said practical Marjorie.

"That's so. Let's trace them and get the wood back."

But after leading away from them for a short distance the

footprints became fainter, and in a softer bit of sand disappeared altogether.

"Pshaw!" said King. "I don't so much care about the wood, but I hate to lose the trail like this. Let's hunt, Mopsy."

"All right, but first, let's bury these apples and potatoes, or they'll be stolen, too."

"Good idea!" And they buried their treasures in the nice, clean sand, and marked the place with an inconspicuous stick.

Then they set out to hunt their lost wood. The beach, though flat and shelving at the water's edge, rose in a low bluff farther back, and this offered among its irregular projections many good hiding-places for their quarry.

And, sure enough, after some searching, they came suddenly upon three boys who sat, shaking with laughter, upon a pile of wood.

The two Maynards glared at them rather angrily, upon which the three again went off in peals of laughter.

"That's our wood!" began King, aggressively.

"Sure it is!" returned the biggest boy, still chuckling.

"What did you bring it over here for?"

"Just for fun!"

"H'm, just for fun! And do you think it would be fun to carry it back again?"

"Yep; just's lieve as not. Come on, kids!" And that remarkable boy began to pick up the sticks.

"Oh, hold on," said King. "If you're so willing, you needn't do it! Who are you, anyway?"

"Well," said the biggest boy, suddenly straightening himself up and bowing politely to Marjorie, "we're your neighbors. We live in that green house next to yours. And we're named Tom, Dick, and Harry. Yes, I know you think those names sound funny, but they're ours all the same. Thomas, Richard, and Henry Craig,—at your service! I'm Tom. This is Dick, and this is Harry."

He whacked his brothers on the shoulder as he named them, and they ducked forward in polite, if awkward salutation.

"And did you really take our wood?" said Marjorie, with an accusing glance, as if surprised that such pleasant-spoken boys could do such a thing.

"Yes, we did. We wanted to see what sort of stuff you were made of. You know Seacote people are sort of like one big family, and we wanted to know how you'd behave about the wood. You've been fine, and now we'll cart it back where we found it. If you had got mad about it, we wouldn't touch a stick to take it back,—would we, fellows?"

"Nope," said the other two, and the Maynards could see at once that Tom was the captain and ringleader of the trio.

"Well," said King, judicially, "if you hadn't been the sort you are, I *should* have got mad. But I guess you're all right, and so you *may* take it back. But we don't help you do it,—see? I'm Kingdon Maynard, and this is my sister Marjorie. You fellows took our wood, and now you're going to return it. Is that right?"

"Right-o!" said Tom. "Come on, fellows."

The three boys flew at it, and King and Midget sat on the sand and watched them till the wood was restored to its original position.

"All right," said King; "you boys'll do. Now, come on and roast potatoes with us."

Thus, all demands of honor having been complied with, the five proceeded to become friends. The boys built the fire, and gallantly let Marjorie have the fun of putting the potatoes and apples in place.

The Craig boys had nice instincts, and while they were rather rough-and-tumble among themselves, they treated King more decorously, and seemed to consider Marjorie as a being of a higher order, made to receive not only respect, but reverent homage.

"You see, we never had a sister," said Tom; "and we're a little bit scared of girls."

"Well, I have three," said King, "so you see I haven't such deep awe of them. But Midget won't hurt you, so don't be *too* scared of her."

Marjorie smiled in most friendly fashion, for she liked these boys, and especially Tom.

"How old are you?" she asked him, in her frank, pleasant way.

"I'm fourteen," replied Tom, "and the other kids are twelve and ten."

"King's fourteen,—'most fifteen," said Midget; "and I'll be thirteen in July. So we're all in the same years. I wish our Kitty was here. She's nearly eleven, but she isn't any bigger than Harry."

Harry smiled shyly, and poked at the potatoes with a stick, not knowing quite what to say.

"You see," King explained, "Midget is the best sort of a girl there is. She's girly, all right, and yet she's as good as a boy at cutting up jinks or doing any old kind of stunts."

The three Craigs looked at Marjorie in speechless admiration.

"I never knew that kind," said Tom, thoughtfully. "You see, we go to a boys' school, and we haven't any girl cousins, or anything; and the only girls I ever see are at dancing class, or in a summer hotel, and then they're all frilled up, and sort of airy."

"I love to play with boys," said Marjorie, frankly, "and I guess we'll have a lot of fun this summer."

"I guess we *will!* Are you going to stay all summer?"

"Yes, till September, when school begins."

"So are we. Isn't it funny we live next door to each other?"

"Awful funny," agreed Marjorie, pulling a very black potato out of the red-hot embers. "This is done," she went on, "and I'm going to eat it."

"So say we all of us," cried King. "One done,—all done! Help yourselves, boys!"

So they all pulled out the black, sooty potatoes, with more delighted anticipations than would have been roused by the daintiest dish served at a table.

"Ow!" cried Marjorie, flinging down her potato, and sticking her finger in her mouth. "Ow! that old thing *popped* open, and burned me awfully!"

"Too bad, Mops!" said King, with genuine sympathy, but the Craig boys were more solicitous.

"Oh, oh! I'm so sorry," cried Tom. "Does it hurt *terribly?*"

"Yes, it does," said Midget, who was not in the habit of complaining when she got hurt, but who was really suffering from the sudden burn.

"Let me tie it up," said Dick, shyly.

"Yes, do," said Tom. "Dick is our good boy. He always helps everybody else."

"But what can we tie it up with?" said Marjorie. "My handkerchief is all black from wiping off that potato."

"I,—I've got a clean one," and Dick, blushing with embarrassment, took a neatly folded white square from his pocket.

"Would you look at that!" said Tom. "I declare Dicky always has the right thing at the right time! Good for you, boy! Fix her up."

Quite deftly Dick wrapped the handkerchief round Marjorie's finger, and secured it with a bit of string from another pocket.

"You ought to have something on it," he said, gravely. "Kerosene is good, but as we haven't any, it will help it just to keep the air away from it, till you go home."

"Goodness!" exclaimed Midget. "You talk like a doctor."

"I'm going to be a doctor when I grow up," said Dick.

"He is," volunteered Harry; "he cured the cat's broken leg, and he mended a bird's wing once."

"Yes, I did," admitted Dick, modestly blushing at his achievements. "Are you going right home because of your finger?"

"No, indeed! We never stop for hurts and things, unless they're bad enough for us to go to bed. Give me another potato, and you open it for me, won't you, Dick?"

"Yep," and Marjorie was immediately supplied with the best of the potatoes and apples, carefully prepared for her use.

"Aren't there any other girls in Seacote?" she inquired.

"There's Hester Corey," answered Tom; "but we don't know her very well. She isn't nice, like you are. And I don't know of any others, though there may be some. Most of the people in the cottages haven't any children,—or else they're grown up,—big girls and young ladies. And there's a few little babies, but not many of our age. So that's why we're so glad you came."

"And that's why you stole our wood!"

"Yes, truly. We thought that'd be a good way to test your temper."

"It was a risky way," said King, thinking it over.

"Oh, I don't know. I knew, if you were the right sort, you'd take it all right; and if you weren't the right sort, we didn't care how you took it."

"That's so," agreed Marjorie.

CHAPTER III

THE SAND CLUB

Life at Seacote soon settled down to its groove, and it was a very pleasant groove. There was always plenty of fun to be had. Bathing every day in the crashing breakers, digging in the sand, building beach fires, talking to the old fishermen, were all delightful pursuits. And then there were long motor rides inland, basket picnics in pine groves, and excursions to nearby watering-places.

The Craig boys turned out to be jolly playfellows, and they and the Maynards became inseparable chums. Marjorie often wished one of them had been a girl, but at the same time, she enjoyed her unique position of being the only girl in the crowd. The boys deferred to her as to a princess, and she ruled them absolutely.

Of course the senior Craigs and Maynards became good friends also, and the two ladies especially spent many pleasant hours together.

Baby Rosamond rarely played with the older children, as she was too little to join in their vigorous games, often original with themselves, and decidedly energetic. The beach was their favorite playground. They never tired of digging in the sand, and they had a multitude of spades and shovels and hoes for their various sand performances. Some days they built a fort, other days a castle or a pleasure ground. Their sand-works were extensive and elaborate, and it often seemed a pity that the tide or the wind should destroy them over night.

"I say, let's us be a Sand Club," said Tom one day. "We're always playing in the sand, you know."

"All right," said Marjorie, instantly seeing delightful possibilities. "We'll call ourselves Sand Crabs, for we're always scrambling through the sand."

"And we're jolly as sandboys!" said King. "I don't know what sandboys really are, but they're always jolly, and so are we."

"I'd like something more gay and festive," Marjorie put in; "I mean like Court Life, or something where we could dress up, and pretend things."

"I know what you mean," said Dick, grasping her idea. "Let's have Sand Court, and build a court and a throne, and we'll all be royal people and Marjorie can be queen."

"Well, let's all have sandy names," suggested Tom. "Marjorie can be Queen Sandy. And we'll call our court Sandringham Palace. You know there is one, really."

"You can be the Grand Sandjandrum!" said King, laughing.

"No, you be that," said Tom, unselfishly.

"No, sir; *you've* got to. I'll be a sand piper, and play the court anthems."

"All right," said Marjorie, "and Harry can be a sand crab, for he just scuttles through the sand all the time. What'll Dick be?"

King looked at Dick. "We'll call him Sandow," he suggested, and they all laughed, for Dick was a frail little chap, without much muscular strength. But the name stuck to him, and they always called him Sandow thereafter.

"I wish we could make our palace where it would stay made," said Marjorie. "We don't want to make a new one every day."

"That's so," said Tom. "If we only could find a secret haunt."

"I know a kind of a one," said Dick; "way back in our yard, near where it joins yours, is a deepy kind of a place, and it's quite sandy."

"Just the thing!" cried Marjorie. "I know that place. Come on!"

She was off like a deer, and the rest followed. A few moments' scamper brought them to the place, and all declared it was just the very spot for a palace.

"I'd like beach sand better, though," said Marjorie.

"We'll bring all you want," declared Tom. "We'll take a wheelbarrow, and bring heaps up from the beach."

The Sand Club worked for days getting their palace in order. The two big boys wheeled many loads of sand up from the beach, and Marjorie and the two other boys arranged it in shape.

Dick was clever at building, and he planned a number of fine effects. Of course, their palace had no roof or walls, but the apartments were partitioned off with low walls of sand, and there were sand sofas and chairs, and a gorgeous throne.

The throne was a heap of sand, surmounted by a legless armchair, found in the Craigs' attic, and at court meetings draped with pink cheesecloth and garlands of flowers. The whole palace was really a "secret haunt," for a slight rise of ground screened it from view on two sides and trees shaded the other side.

Carolyn Wells

The parents of both families were pleased with the whole scheme, for it kept the children occupied, and they could always be found at a moment's notice.

Sand tables were built, and on them were bits of old dishes and broken vases, all of which were desirable because they could stay out in the rain and not be harmed. Moreover, they were handy in case of a feast. At last preparations were complete and they decided to open the court next day.

"We must have a flag," said Marjorie. "I'll make it. The court colors are red and yellow, and our emblem will be,—what shall our emblem be?"

"A pail of sand," suggested Tom.

"Yes; I can cut out a pail of red flannel, and sew it on to a yellow flag. I'll make that this afternoon, and we'll hold court to-morrow morning at ten o'clock. We must all wear some red and yellow. Sashes will do for you boys, and I'll have,—well, I'll fix up a rig of some kind."

Marjorie was a diligent little worker when she chose to be, and that afternoon she made a very creditable flag, showing a pail, red; on a field, yellow. She made also sashes for them all, of red and yellow cheesecloth, and she made herself a court train of the same material, which trailed grandly from her shoulders.

Next morning the Sand Club assembled on the Maynards' veranda, to march to Sandringham Palace.

Mrs. Craig had helped out the costumes of her royal children, and the Grand Sandjandrum was gorgeous in a voluminous yellow turban, with a red cockade sticking up on one side.

Sandow and the Sand Crab had soldier hats made of red and yellow paper, and big sailor collars of the same colors.

The Sand Piper wore his sash jauntily with a huge shoulder

knot, and he, too, had a cockaded headgear.

Marjorie, as Queen Sandy, wore her trailing court robe and a crown of yellow paper with red stars on it. She had a sceptre, and Sandow carried the flag.

The Sand Piper marched ahead, playing on a tuneful instrument known as a kazoo. Next came the Grand Sandjandrum, then the Queen, then the Sand Crab, and finally, Sandow with the flag.

Slowly and with great dignity the procession filed out toward the palace. King was playing the Star Spangled Banner, or thought he was. It sounded almost as much like Hail Columbia,—but it didn't really matter, and they're both difficult tunes, anyway.

Blithely they stepped along, and prepared to enter the palace with a flourish of trumpets, as it were, when King's music stopped suddenly.

"Great Golliwogs!" he cried. "Look at that!"

"Look at what?" said Tom, who was absorbed in the grand march.

But he looked, and they all looked, and five angry exclamations sounded as they saw only the ruins of the beloved Sandringham Palace.

Somebody had utterly demolished it. The low walls were broken and scattered, the sand tables and chairs were torn down, and the throne was entirely upset.

"Who did this?" roared Tom.

But as nobody knew the answer, there was no reply.

"It couldn't have been any of your servants, could it?" asked

Carolyn Wells

King of the Craigs. "I know it wasn't any of ours."

"No; it wasn't ours, either," said Tom. "Could it have been your little sister?"

"Mercy, no!" cried Marjorie. "Rosy Posy isn't that sort of a child. Oh, I do think it's awful!" and forgetting her royal dignity, Queen Sandy began to cry.

"Why, Mops," said King, kindly; "brace up, old girl. Don't cry."

"I'm not a cry baby," said Midget, smiling through her tears. "I'm just crying 'cause I'm so *mad*! I'm mad clear through! How *could* anybody be so ugly?"

"I'm mad, too," declared Tom, slowly, "but I know who did it, and it's partly my fault, I s'pose."

"Your fault!" exclaimed Midget. "Why, Tom, how can it be?"

"Well, you see it was this way. Yesterday afternoon Mrs. Corey came to call on my mother, and she brought Hester with her."

"That red-headed girl?"

"Yes; and she has a temper to match her hair! Mother made me talk to her, and, as I didn't know what else to talk about, I told her about our Sand Club, and about the Court to-day and everything. And she wanted to belong to the club, and I told her she couldn't, because it was just the Maynards and the Craigs. And she was madder'n hops, and she coaxed me, and I still said no, and then she said she'd get even with us somehow."

"But, Tom," said King, "we don't know that girl to speak to. We hardly know her by sight."

"But we do. We knew her when we were here last summer,

but, you see, this year we've had you two to play with, so we've sort of neglected her,—and she doesn't like it."

"But that's no reason she should spoil our palace," and Marjorie looked sadly at the scene of ruin and destruction.

"No; and of course I'm not sure that she did do it. But she said she'd do something to get even with you."

"With me? Why, she doesn't know me at all."

"That's what she's mad about. She says you're stuck up, and you put on airs and never look at her."

"Why, how silly! I don't know her, but somehow, from her looks, I *know* I shouldn't like her."

"No, you wouldn't, Marjorie. She's selfish, and she's ill-tempered. She flies into a rage at any little thing, and,—well, she isn't a bit like you Maynards."

"*No!* and I'm glad of it! I wouldn't *want* to be like such a stuck-up thing!"

These last words were spoken by a strange voice, and Marjorie looked round quickly to see a shock of red hair surmounting a very angry little face just appearing from behind the small hill, beneath whose overhanging shadow they had built their palace.

"Why, Hester Corey!" shouted Tom. "What are you doing here?"

"I came to see how you like your old sand-house!" she jeered, mockingly, and making faces at Marjorie between her words. Marjorie was utterly astonished. It was her first experience with a child of this type, and she didn't know just how to take her.

The newcomer was a little termagant. Her big blue eyes seemed to flash with anger, and as she danced about, shaking her fist at Marjorie and pointing her forefinger at her, she cried, tauntingly, "Stuck up! Proudy!"

Marjorie grew indignant. She had done nothing knowingly to provoke this wrath, so she faced the visitor squarely, and glared back at her.

"I'd rather be stuck up than to be such a spiteful thing as you are!" she declared. "Did *you* tear down this palace that we took such trouble to build?"

"Yes, I did!" said Hester. "And if you build it again, I'll tear it down again,—so, there, now!"

"You'll do no such thing!" shouted Tom.

"Huh, Smarty! What have you got to say about it?"

The crazy little Hester flew at Tom and pounded him vigorously on the back.

"I hate you!" she cried. "I *hate* you!"

As a matter of fact, her little fists couldn't hurt the big, sturdy boy, but her intense anger made him angry too.

"You, Hester Corey!" he cried. "You leave me alone!"

King stood a little apart, with his hands in his pockets, looking at the combatants.

"Say, we've had about enough of this," he said, speaking quietly, and without excitement. "We Maynards are not accustomed to this sort of thing. We squabble sometimes, but we never get really angry."

"Goody-goody boy!" said Hester, sneeringly, and making one of her worst faces at him. For some reason this performance struck King as funny.

"Do it again," he said. "How do you ever squink up your nose like that! Bet you can't do it three times in succession."

The audacious Hester tried it, and the result was so ludicrous they all laughed.

"Now look here," went on King, "we're not acquainted with you, but we know you're Hester Corey. We know you spoiled our Sand Palace, just out of angry spite. Now, Hester Corey, you've got to be punished for that. We're peaceable people ourselves, but we're just, also. We were about to have a nice celebration, but you've put an end to that before it began. So, instead, we're going to have a trial. You're the prisoner, and you've pleaded guilty,—at least, you've confessed your crime. Queen Sandy, get into that throne,—never mind if it is upset,—set it up again. Grand Sandjandrum, take your place on that mussed up sand heap. You two other chaps,—stand one each side of the prisoner as sentinels. I'll conduct this case, and Queen Sandy will pronounce the sentence. It's us Maynards that Hester Corey seems to have a grudge against, so it's up to us Maynards to take charge of the case. Prisoner, stand on that board there."

"I won't do it!" snapped Hester, and the red locks shook vigorously.

"You will do it," said King, quietly, and for some reason or other Hester quailed before his glance, and then meekly stood where he told her to.

"Have you anything to say for yourself?" King went on. "Any excuse to offer for such a mean, hateful piece of work?"

Hester sulked a minute, then she said:

"Yes, I was mad at you, because you all have such good times, and wouldn't let me in them."

"What do you mean by that? You never asked to come in."

"I did. I asked Tom Craig yesterday, and he wouldn't ask you."

"Then why are you mad at us?"

"Because you're so proud and exclusive. You think yourselves so great; you think nobody's as good as you are!"

"That isn't true, Hester," said King, quite gently; "and even if it were, are you proving yourself better than we are by cutting up this mean, babyish trick? If you want us to like you, why not make yourself likeable, instead of horrid and hateful?"

This was a new idea to Hester, and she stared at King as if greatly interested.

"That's right," he went on. "If people want people to like them, they must be likeable. They must be obliging and kind and pleasant, and not small and spiteful."

"You haven't been very nice to me," muttered Hester.

"We haven't had a chance. And before we get a chance you upset everything by making us dislike you! What kind of common sense is that?"

"Maybe you could forgive me," suggested Hester, hopefully.

"Maybe we could, later on. But we're for fair play, and you treated us unfairly. So now, you've got to be punished. Queen Sandy, Grand Sandjandrum, which of you can suggest proper punishment for this prisoner of ours?"

Tom thought for a moment, then he said:

"Seems 's if she ought to put this palace back in order, just as it was when she found it,—but that's too hard work for a girl."

"I'll help her," said Harry, earnestly. "I'm sorry for her."

"Sorry for her!" cried Tom, with blazing eyes. "*Sorry* for the girl that spoiled our palace!"

"Well, you see," went on Harry, "she's sorry herself now."

CHAPTER IV

SAND COURT

With one accord, they all looked at Hester. Sure enough, it was easily to be seen that she was sorry. All her anger and rage had vanished, and she stood digging one toe into the sand, and twisting from side to side, with her eyes cast down, and two big tears rolling slowly down her cheeks.

Marjorie sprang up from her wabbly throne, and running to Hester, threw her arms around her.

"Don't cry, Hester," she said. "We'll all forgive you. I think you lost your temper and I think you're sorry now, aren't you?"

"Oh, yes, yes, I am!" sobbed Hester. "But I envied the good times you had, and when Tom wouldn't let me into your club, I got so mad I didn't know what to do."

"There, there, don't cry any more," and Midget smoothed the tangled red mop, and tried to comfort the bad little Hester.

Tom looked rather disappointed.

"I say," he began, "she did an awful mean thing, and she ought to be—"

"Hold on a minute, Tom," said Marjorie. "I'm Queen of this

club, and what I say goes! Is that right, my courtiers?"

She looked round at the boys, smiling in a wheedlesome way, and King said, "Right, O Queen Sandy! Right always and ever, in the hearts of your gentlemen-in-waiting."

"You bet you are!" cried Tom, quick to follow King's lead. "Our noble Queen has but to say the word, and it is our law. Therefore, O Queen, we beg thee to mete out a just punishment to this prisoner within our gates."

"Hear ye! Hear ye!" said Midget, with great dramatic fervor. "I hereby forgive this prisoner of ours, because she's truly sorry she acted like the dickens. And as a punishment, I condemn her to rebuild this royal palace, but, following Harry's example, we will all help her with the work."

Then King burst forth into song:

"Hooray, Hooray, for our noble Queen,
The very best monarch that ever was seen.
There's nobody quite so perfectly dandy,
As our most gracious, most noble Queen Sandy!"

They all repeated this chorus, and the Queen bowed and smiled at her devoted court.

"And also," her Royal Highness went on, "we hereby take into our club Miss Hester Corey as a new member. I'm glad to have another girl in it,—and what I say goes!"

This time Tom made up the song:

"What she says, goes!
She's sweet as a rose,
From head to toes,
So what she says, goes!"

"Miss Hester Corey is now a member," said Midget, "and her

name is,—is—"

"Sand Witch," suggested Tom.

"Yes," said King; "you expect witches to cut up tricks."

"All right," said Hester. "Call me Sand Witch, and you'll see there are good witches as well as bad."

"Come on, then," said Marjorie, "and show us how you can work. Let's put this palace back into shape again as quick as scat!"

They all fell to work, and it didn't take so very long after all. Hester was conquered by the power of Marjorie's kindness, and she was meek as a lamb. She did whatever she was told, and was a quick and willing worker.

"Now," said Midget, after it was all in order once more, "now we'll have our celebration. You see, we have six in our court now, instead of five, and I think it's nicer. I'll give the Sand Witch my sash to wear, and she can be my first lady-in-waiting."

This position greatly pleased Hester, and she took her place at the side of the enthroned Queen, while Tom stood at her other side. King played a grand tune, and they all sang.

The song was in honor of the flag-raising, and was hastily composed by Marjorie for the occasion:

> "Our Flag, our Flag, our Sand Club Flag!
> Long may she wave, long may she wag!
> And may our Sand Club ever stand
> A glory to our Native Land."

Tom persisted in singing "a glory to our native *sand*," and King said *strand*, but after all, it didn't matter.

Then Sandow, bearing the flag, stepped gravely forward, and the boys all helped to plant it firmly in the middle of Sand Court, while the Queen and her lady-in-waiting nodded approval.

"Ha, Courtiers! I prithee sit!" the Queen commanded, when the flag was gaily waving in the breeze.

Her four courtiers promptly sat on the ground at her feet, and the Queen addressed them thus:

"Gentlemen-in-waiting of Sandringham Palace, there are much affairs of state now before us. First must we form our club, our Sand Club."

"Most noble Queen," and Tom rose to his feet, "have I your permission to speak?"

"Speak!" said the Queen, graciously, waving her sceptre at him.

"Then I rise to inquire if this is a secret organization."

"You bet it is!" cried King, jumping up. "The very secretest ever! If any one lets out the secrets of these secret meetings, he shall be excommunicated in both feet!"

"A just penalty!" said Tom, gravely.

"Is all well, O fair Queen? Do you agree?"

"Yes, I agree," said the Queen, smiling. "But I want to know what these secrets are to be about."

"That's future business," declared King. "Just now we have to elect officers, and all that."

"All right," said Marjorie, "but you must be more courtly about it. Say it more,—you know how I mean."

"As thus," spoke up the lady-in-waiting, dropping on one knee before the Queen.

"What is the gracious will of your Royal Highness in the matter of secretary and treasurer, O Queen!"

"Yes, that's better. Well, my court, to tell you the truth, I don't think that we need a secretary and such things, because it isn't a regular club. Let us content ourselves with our present noble offices. Grand Sandjandrum, what are the duties of thy high office?"

"No duties, but all pleasures, when serving thee, O noble and gracious Queen!"

"That's fine," said Midget, clapping her hands. "Hither, Sir Sand Piper! What are thy duties at, court?"

"Your Majesty," said King, bowing low, "it is my humble part to play the pipes, or to lay the pipes, as the case may be. I do not smoke pipes, but, if it be thy gracious wish, I can blow fair soap bubbles from them."

"Sand Piper, I see you know your business," said the Queen. "Ha! Sand Crab, what dost thou do each day?"

"Just scramble around in the sand," replied Harry, and suiting the action to the word, he gave such a funny scrambling performance that they all applauded.

"Right well done, noble Sand Crab," commented the smiling Queen. "And thou, O Sandow?"

"I do all the strong-arm work required in the palace," said Dick, doubling up his little fist, and trying to make it look large and powerful.

"Now, thee, my fair lady-in-waiting, what dost thou do in this, my court?"

Hester shook back her mop of red curls, and her eyes danced as she answered, gaily:

"I am the Court Sand Witch! I cut up tricks of all sorts, as doth become a witch. Aye, many a time will I cause enchantments to fall upon thee, one and all! I am a magic witch, and I can cast spells!"

Hester waved her arms about, and swayed from side to side, her eyes fixed in a glassy stare, and her red curls bobbing.

"Good gracious!" cried Marjorie. "You're like a witch I saw on the stage once in a fairy pantomime. Say, Hester, let's have a pantomime entertainment some day."

"All right. My mother'll help us. She's always getting up private theatricals and things like that. She says I inherit her dramatic talent."

"All right," said Tom, warningly; "but don't you turn your dramatic talent toward tearing down our palace again."

"Of course I won't, now I'm a member."

"Of course she won't," agreed Marjorie. "Now, my courtiers, and lady-in-waiting, there's another subject to come before your royal attention. We must have a Court Journal."

"What's that?" inquired Harry.

"Why, a sort of a paper, you know, with all the court news in it."

"There isn't any."

"But there will be. We're not fairly started yet. Now who'll write this paper?"

"All of us," suggested Tom.

"Yes; but there must be one at the head of it,—sort of editor, you know."

"Guess it better be King," said Tom, thoughtfully. "He knows the most about writing things."

"All right," agreed King. "I'll edit the paper, only you must all contribute. We'll have it once a week, and everybody must send me some contribution, if it's only a little poem or something."

"I can't write poems," said Harry, earnestly, "but I can gather up news,—and like that."

"Yes," said Marjorie, "that's what I mean. But it must be news about us court people, or maybe our families."

"Can't we make it up?" asked Hester.

"Yes, I s'pose so, if you make it real court like and grand sounding."

"What shall we call our paper?" asked King.

"Oh, just the *Court Journal*," replied Midget.

"I don't think so," objected Hester. "I think it ought to have a name like *The Sand Club*."

"*The Jolly Sandboy*," exclaimed Tom. "How's that?"

"But two of us are girls!" said Marjorie.

"That doesn't matter, it's just the name of the paper, you know. And it sounds so gay and jolly."

"I like it," declared King, and so they all agreed to the name.

"Now, my courtiers and noble friends," said their Queen, "it's time we all scooted home to luncheon. My queen-dowager mother likes me to be on time for meals. Also, my majesty and my royal sand piper can't come back to play this afternoon. But shall this court meet to-morrow morning?"

"You bet, your Majesty!" exclaimed Tom, with fervor.

"That isn't very courtly language, my Grand Sandjandrum."

"I humbly beg your Majesty's pardon, and I prostrate myself in humble humility!" And Tom sprawled on his face at Marjorie's feet.

"Rise, Sir Knight," said the gracious Queen, and then the court dispersed toward its various homes.

"Well, we had the greatest time this morning you ever heard of!" announced Marjorie as, divested of her royal trappings and clad in a fresh pink gingham, she sat at the luncheon table.

"What was it all about, Moppets?" asked Mrs. Maynard.

So King and Marjorie together told all about the intrusion of Hester on their celebration, and how they had finally taken her into the Sand Club as a member.

"I think my children behaved very well," said Mrs. Maynard, looking at the two with pride.

"I did get sort of mad at first, Mother," Marjorie confessed, not wanting more praise than was her just due.

"Well, I don't blame you!" declared King. "Why, that girl made most awful faces at Mops, and talked to her just horrid! If she hadn't calmed down afterward we couldn't have played with her at all."

"I've heard about that child," said Mrs. Maynard. "She has most awful fits of temper, I'm told. Mrs. Craig says that Hester will be as good and as sweet as a lamb for days,—and then she'll fly into a rage over some little thing. I'm glad you children are not like that."

"I'm glad, too," said King. "We're not angels, but if we acted up like Hester did at first we couldn't live in the house with each other!"

"Her mother is an actress," observed Marjorie.

"Oh, no, Midget, you're mistaken," said her mother. "I know Mrs. Corey, and she isn't an actress at all, and never was. But she is fond of amateur theatricals, and she is president of a club that gives little plays now and then."

"Yes, that's it," said King. "Hester said her mother had dramatic talent, and she had inherited it. Have you dramatic talent, Mother?"

"I don't know, King," said Mrs. Maynard, laughing. "Your father and I have joined their dramatic club, but it remains to be seen whether we can make a success of it."

"Oh, Mother!" cried Marjorie. "Are you really going to act in a play? Oh, can we see you?"

"I don't know yet, Midget. Probably it will be an entertainment only for grown-ups. We've just begun rehearsals."

"Have we dramatic talent, Mother?"

"Not to any astonishing degree. But, yes, I suppose your fondness for playing at court life and such things shows a dramatic taste."

"Oh, it's great fun, Mother! I just love to sit on that throne with my long trail wopsed on the floor beside me, and my sceptre sticking up, and my courtiers all around me,—oh, Mother, I think I'd like to be a real queen!"

"Well, you see, Midget, you were born in a country that doesn't employ queens."

"And I'm glad of it!" cried Marjorie, patriotically. "Hooray! for the land of the free and the home of the brave! I guess I don't care to be a real queen, I guess I'll be a president's wife instead. Say, Mother, won't you and Father write us some poems for *The Jolly Sandboy*?"

"What is that, Midget?"

"Oh, it's our court journal,—and you and Father do write such lovely poetry. Will you, Mother?"

"Yes, I 'spect so."

"Oh, goody! When you say 'I 'spect so,' you always *do*. Hey, King, Rosy Posy ought to have a sandy kind of a name, even if she doesn't come to our court meetings."

"'Course she ought. And she can come sometimes, if she doesn't upset things."

"She can't upset things worse'n Hester did."

"No; but I don't believe Hester will act up like that again."

"She may, Marjorie," said Mrs. Maynard. "I've heard her mother say she can't seem to curb Hester's habit of flying into a temper. So just here, my two loved ones, let me ask you to be kind to the little girl, and if she gets angry, don't flare back at her, but try 'a soft answer.'"

"But, Mother," said King, "that isn't so awful easy! And, anyway, I don't think she ought to do horrid things,—like tumbling down our palace,—and then we just forgive her, and take her into the club!"

"Why not, King?"

Carolyn Wells

King looked a little nonplussed.

"Why," he said, "why,—because it doesn't seem fair."

"And does it seem fairer for you to lose your temper too, and try what children call 'getting even with her'?"

"Well, Mother, it *does* seem fairer, but I guess it isn't very,—very *noble*."

"No, son, it isn't. And I hope you'll come to think that sometimes nobility of action is better than mere justice."

"I see what you mean, Mother, and somehow, talking here with you, it all seems true enough. But when we get away from you, and off with the boys and girls, these things seem different. Were you always noble when you were little, Mother?"

"No, Kingdon dear, I wasn't always. But my mother tried her best to teach me to be,—so don't you think I ought to try to teach you?"

"Sure, Mothery! And you bet we'll do our bestest to try to learn. Hey, Mops?"

"Yes, indeedy! I *want* to do things right, but I seem to forget just when I ought to remember."

"Well, when you forget, come home and tell Mother all about it, and we'll take a fresh start. You're pretty fairly, tolerably, moderately good children after all! Only I want you to grow a little speck better each day."

"And we *will*!" shouted King and Marjorie together.

CHAPTER V

"THE JOLLY SANDBOY"

The Sand Club was not very strict in its methods or systems. Some days it met, and some days it didn't. Sometimes all the court was present, and sometimes only three or four of them.

But everything went on harmoniously, and there were no exhibitions of ill temper from the Sand Witch.

In fact, Hester was absorbed in doing her part toward the first number of *The Jolly Sandboy*.

The child was quite an adept at drawing and painting, and she was making several illustrations for their court journal. One, representing Marjorie seated on her sand throne, was really clever, and there were other smaller pictures, too.

Kingdon worked earnestly to get the paper into shape. He had contributions from all the club, and from Mr. and Mrs. Maynard also. He had a small typewriter of his own, and he laboriously copied the contributions on fair, white pages, and, with Hester's pictures interspersed, bound them all into a neat cover of red paper.

This Hester ornamented with a yellow sand-pail, emblem of their club, and tied it at the top with a yellow ribbon. Altogether, the first number of *The Jolly Sandboy* was a strikingly beautiful affair.

And the court convened, in full court dress, to hear it read.

The court wardrobes had received various additions. Often a courtier blossomed out in some new regalia, always of red or yellow, or both.

The several mothers of the court frequently donated old ribbons, feathers, or flowers, from discarded millinery or other finery, and all these were utilized by the frippery loving courtiers.

Hester had contrived a witch costume, which was greatly admired. A red skirt, a yellow shawl folded cornerwise, and a very tall peaked hat of black with red and yellow ribbons, made the child look like some weird creature.

Marjorie's tastes ran rather to magnificent attire, and she accumulated waving plumes, artificial flowers, and floating gauze veils and draperies.

The boys wore nondescript costumes, in which red jerseys and yellow sashes played a prominent part, while King achieved the dignity of a mantle, picturesquely slung from one shoulder. Many badges and orders adorned their breasts, and lances and spears, wound with gilt paper, added to the courtly effect.

"My dearly beloved Court," Marjorie began, beaming graciously from her flower decked throne, "we are gathered together here to-day to listen to the reading of our Court Journal,—a noble paper,—published by our noble courtier, the Sand Piper, who will now read it to us."

"Hear! Hear!" cried all the courtiers.

"Most liege Majesty," began King, bowing so low that his shoulder cape fell off. But he hastily swung it back into place and went on. "Also, most liege lady-in-waiting, our noble Sand Witch, we greet thee. And we greet our Grand Sandjandrum, and our noble Sandow, and our beloved Sand Crab. We greet all, and everybody. Did I leave anybody out of this greeting?"

"No! No!"

"All right; then I'll fire away. The first article in this paper is an editorial,—I wrote it myself because I am editor-in-chief. You're all editors, you know, but I'm the head editor."

"Why not say headitor?" suggested Tom.

"Good idea, friend Courtier! I'm the headitor, then. And this is my headitorial. Here goes! 'Courtiers and Citizens: This journal, called *The Jolly Sandboy*, shall relate from time to time the doings of our noble court. It shall tell of the doughty deeds of our brave knights, and relate the gay doings of our fair ladies. It shall mention news of interest, if any, concerning the inhabitants of Seacote in general, and the families of this court in particular. Our politics are not confined to any especial party, but our platform is to grow up to be presidents ourselves.' This ends my headitorial."

Great applause followed this masterpiece of journalistic literature, and the Sand Piper proceeded:

"I will next read the column of news, notes, and social events, as collected by our energetic and capable young reporter, the Sand Crab:

* * * * *

The Queen and her lady-in-waiting went bathing in the ocean this morning. Our noble Queen was costumed in white, trimmed with blue, and the Sand Witch in dark blue trimmed with red. Both noble ladies squealed when a large breaker knocked them over. The whole court rushed to their rescue, and no permanent damage resulted.

"Three gentlemen courtiers of this court, who reside in the same castle, had ice-cream for dinner last night. The colors were pink and white. It was exceeding good.

"A very young princess, a sister of our beloved Queen, went walking yesterday afternoon with her maid of honor. The princess wore a big white hat with funny ribbon bunches on it. Also white shoes.

"Mr. Sears has had his back fence painted. (We don't know any Mr. Sears, and he hasn't any back fence, but we are making up now, as our real news has given out and our column isn't full.)

"Mrs. Black spent Sunday with her mother-in-law, Mrs. Green. (See above.)

"Mr. Van Winkle is building a gray stone mansion of forty rooms on Seashore Drive. We think it is quite a pretty house.

"This is all the news I can find for this time. Yours truly. —THE SAND CRAB.'"

*   *   *   *   *

"Noble Sand Crab, we thank you for your fine contribution to our midst," announced the Queen, and the Sand Crab burrowed in the sand and kicked in sheer delight at such praise.

"The next," announced the Sand Piper, "is an original poem by our most liege majesty, the Queen. It's pretty fine, I think.

> "Most noble Court, I greet you now,
> From Grand Sandjandrum to small Sandow.
> From old Sand Piper, and gay Sand Witch,
> To Sand Crab, with hair as black as pitch.
> I hope our Court will ever be
> Renowned for its fun and harmony.
> And as I gaze on this gorgeous scene,
> I'm glad I am your beloved Queen."

"Jinks! that's gay!" exclaimed Tom. "How do you ever do it, Marjorie? I did a poem, but it doesn't run nice and slick like yours."

"I'll read it next," said King. "I think it's pretty good.

"I love the people named *Maynard*,
I like to play in their back yard.
We have a jolly Sand Court,
Which makes the time fly very short.
Except going in the ocean bathing,
There's nothing I like so much for a plaything."

"That's very nice, Tom," said Marjorie, forgetting her role.

"No, it isn't. It seems as if it ought to be right, and then somehow it isn't. Bathing and plaything are 'most alike, and yet they sound awful different."

"That's so. Well, anyway, it's plenty good enough, and it's all true, Tom."

"Yes, it's all true."

"Then it must be right, 'cause there's a quotation or something that says truth is beauty. We wouldn't want all our poems to be just alike, you know."

"No, I s'pose not," and Tom felt greatly encouraged by Marjorie's kind criticism.

"Next," said King, "is our Puzzle Department. It's sort of queer, but it's Sandow's contribution, and he said to put it in, and he'd explain about it. So here it is.

* * * * *

"SANDY PRIZE PUZZLE. Prize, a musical top, donated by the author. Question: Is the number of sands on the seashore odd or even? Anybody in this court who can answer this question truthfully will receive the prize. Signed, SANDOW."

* * * * *

"That's nonsense," cried Hester. "How can anybody tell whether we answer truthfully or not?"

"I can tell," said Sandow, gravely. "Whoever first answers it truthfully will get the prize."

"But it's ridiculous," said King. "In the first place, how much seashore do you mean? Only that here at Seacote, or all the Atlantic shore? Or all the world?"

Dick considered. "I mean all the seashore in all the world," he said, at last.

"Then that's silly, too," said Tom, "for how far does the seashore go? Just to the edge of the ocean, or all the way under?"

"All the way under," replied Dick, solemnly.

"Then you really mean all the sand in all the world!"

"Yes; that's it. Of course, all the sand in all the world numbers a certain number of grains. Now, is that number odd or even?"

"You're crazy, Dick!" said Hester, but Marjorie said, "No, he isn't crazy; I think there's a principle there somewhere, but I can't work it out."

"I guess you can't!" said King. "I give it up."

"So do I!" declared Tom, and at last they all gave it up.

"Now you must answer it yourself, Dick," said King.

"Then nobody gets the prize," objected Sandow.

"No, you keep it yourself. Have you got one, anyhow?"

"Yes, a nice musical top Uncle John sent to me. I've never used it much, it's as good as new. I *wish* somebody would guess."

Nobody did, and Dick sighed.

"Bet you can't answer your old puzzle, yourself," said Hester.

"Yes, I can," averred Dick, "but you must ask it to me."

"All right," said King. "Mr. Sandow, honorable and noble courtier of Sand Court, is the number of sea sands odd or even? Answer truthfully now."

"I don't know," replied Dick, "and that's the truth!"

How they all laughed! It was a quibble, of course, but the Maynard children were surprised at themselves that they hadn't seen through the catch.

Dick sat on the sand, rocking back and forth with laughter.

"The witch ought to have guessed it," he cried; "or else the Queen ought to."

"Yes, my courtier, we ought," Marjorie admitted. "You caught us fairly, and we hereby give you the post of wizard of this court. Sand Piper, what's next in your journal?"

"The next is a poem by the Honorable Edward Maynard. That is, he wrote part of it, and then, as he had to go to New York on business, his honorable wife finished it. Here it is:

"Royal Courtiers, great and grand,
Ruling o'er your court of sand,
Take this greeting from the pen

Of an humble citizen.
May you, each one, learn to be
Filled with true nobility;
Gentle, loving, brave, and kind,
Strong of arm and pure of mind.
May you have a lot of fun,
And look back, when day is done,
O'er long hours of merry play
Filled with laughter blithe and gay.
May your court of mimic rule
Teach you lore not learned in school;
Rule your heart to think no ill,
Rule your temper and your will."

"Gee, that's real poetry, that is!" exclaimed Tom. "Say, your people are poets, aren't they?"

"Why, I think they are," said Marjorie, "but Father says they're not."

"I'd like a copy of that poem," said Hester, looking very serious.

"All right," said King, catching the witch's glance. "I'll make you a nice typewritten copy of it to-morrow."

"And now, my royal Sand Piper, is there any more poetic lore for us to listen to?"

"Aye, my liege Queen, there is one more poem. This is a real poem also, but it is of the humorous variety. It was composed by the mother of our royal Sand Witch, and was freely contributed to our paper by that estimable lady. Methinks she mistook our club for a debating club, and yet, perhaps not. This may be merely a flight of fancy, such as poets are very fond of, I am told. I will now read Mrs. Corey's contribution:

"There once was a Debating Club, exceeding wise and great; On grave and abstruse questions it would eagerly debate. Its members said: 'We are so wise, ourselves we'll herewith dub The Great Aristophelean Pythagoristic Club.' And every night these bigwigs met, and strove with utmost pains To solve recondite problems that would baffle lesser brains. They argued and debated till the hours were small and wee; And weren't much discouraged if they didn't then agree. They said their say, and went their way, these cheerful, pleasant men, And then came round next evening, and said it all again. Well, possibly, you'll be surprised; but all the winter through The questions they debated on numbered exactly two. For as they said: 'Of course we can't take up another one, Till we have solved conclusively the two that we've begun.' They reasoned and they argued, as the evenings wore along; And each one thought that he was right, and deemed the others wrong. They wrangled and contended, they disputed and discussed, They retorted and rebutted, they refuted and they fussed; But though their wisdom was profound, and erudite their speech, A definite conclusion those men could never reach. And so the club disbanded, and they read their last report, Which told the whole sad story, though it was exceeding short: 'Resolved— We are not able to solve these problems two: "Does Polly want a cracker?" and "What did Katy do?"'"

"Well, isn't that fine!" cried Marjorie. "Why, Hester, your mother is more a poet than ours."

"She does write lovely poetry," said Hester, "but I like your mother's poem, too, because it,—well, you know what I mean."

Somehow the children all understood that tempestuous Hester appreciated the lines that so gently advised the ruling and subduing of an unruly temper and will, but nobody knew just how to express it.

So King broke a somewhat awkward silence by saying, heartily, "Yep, we know!" and all the others said "Yep" in chorus.

Carolyn Wells

"I think, O Royal Court," the Queen began, "that our first paper is fine. How often shall we issue *The Jolly Sandboy*?"

"'Bout once a week, I think," said Tom.

"All right," agreed King; "and you fellows get your stuff in a little earlier next week so's I can typewrite it in time."

"And now, my beloved court," resumed Midget, "I think we have sat still long enough, and I decree that we have a game of Prisoner's Base. And what I say goes!"

There was no dissenting voice. The Queen unpinned her court train from her shoulders, the Sand Witch laid aside her tall, peaked hat, and the courtiers discarded such details of their costumes as seemed likely to impede progress in the game. Prisoner's Base was followed by Hide and Seek, and then it was time for the court to repair to its several homes.

"It's all so lovely, Marjorie," said Hester. "I'm *so* glad you let me play with you."

"That's all right, Hester, as long as you don't smash things or make faces at us."

"Oh, I never will again; truly, Marjorie. I'm going to learn that poem of your mother's by heart, and I *know* I'll never lose my temper again, Good-bye."

"Good-bye, Hester," and after an affectionate kiss the two girls parted.

"Goo'-bye, Queenie Sandy," called Tom, as they separated at the turn of the path.

"Good-bye, Tom, you old Grand Sandjandrum!" and then the Maynards ran into their own house.

"Gently, my lad and lassie; gently!" warned Mrs. Maynard, as her two young hopefuls flung themselves upon her.

"Oh, Mothery," cried Marjorie, "we had *such* a good time! And our court journal was lovely! Want to see it? And King fixed it up so beautifully, and Hester made such *dear* pictures for it! Oh, Mother, isn't it splendid to have so much fun?"

"Yes, dearie," and Mrs. Maynard stroked the flushed brow of her energetic and excitable daughter. "But when you come in from your play, you must be a little bit quieter and more ladylike. I don't want to think that these merry companions of yours are making you really boisterous."

"They are, though," said King. "I like the Craigs and Hester Corey, but they sure are the noisy bunch!"

"Oh, King, not *quite* so much slang!"

"No, Mother, we won't get gay! We'll try to please you every way! But we're feeling rather spry to-day! So please excuse us, Mothery May!"

CHAPTER VI

TWO WELCOME GUESTS

It was Saturday afternoon. The Maynard children had been told that guests were expected to dinner, and they must put on festival array.

And so when King and Marjorie, in white serge and white pique respectively, wandered out on to the front veranda, they found their parents and a very dressy-looking Rosamond there before them.

"Who are coming to dinner, Mother?" asked Midget.

"Ask your father, my dear."

"Why, don't *you* know, Mother? Well, who are they, Daddy?"

"Somebody and somebody else," replied Mr. Maynard, smiling.

"Oho, a secret!" exclaimed Midget. "Then it must be somebody nice! Let's guess, King."

"All right. Are they kids or grown-ups, Father?"

"Grown-ups, my son."

"Oh!" and Marjorie looked disappointed. "Do we

know them?"

"You have met them, yes."

"Do they live at Seacote?"

"They are here for the summer."

"Where do they live winters?" asked King.

"Under the Stars and Stripes."

"Huh! that may mean the Philippines or Alaska!"

"It may. Have you met many people who reside in those somewhat removed spots?"

"Not many," said King, "and that's a fact. Well, are they a lady and gentleman?"

"They are."

"Oh, I know!" cried Marjorie. "It's Kitty and Uncle Steve! He said they'd come down here some time while we're here! Am I right, Father?"

"Not quite, Mopsy. You see, I said they are grown-ups."

"Both of them?"

"Both of them."

"Well, I don't care much who they are, then," declared King. "I don't see anything in it for us, Mops."

"No, but we ought to guess them if they're spending the summer here and we've met them. Of course, it couldn't be Kitty! She isn't spending the summer here. Is it the Coreys or Craigs, Father?"

"No, neither of those names fit our expected guests."

"Then it must be some of those people the other side of the pier. I don't know any more on this side except the fishermen. Is it any of them?"

"Well, no. I doubt if they'd care to visit us. But never mind our guests for the moment; I want you two children to go on an errand for me."

"Right-o!" said King. "Where?"

"Walk along the shore road three blocks, then turn inland and walk a block and a half. Do you know that place with lots of vines all over the front of the house?"

"Yes, I do," said Marjorie, "but nobody lives there."

"All right. I want you to take a message to Mr. Nobody."

"Oh, Father, what do you mean?"

"Just what I say. You say nobody lives there, and that's the very man I mean."

"All right," said King. "We'll go, if you tell us to. Hey, Mops?"

"'Course we will! What shall we say to Mr. Nobody, Father?"

"First you must ring the doorbell, and if Nobody opens the door, walk in."

"Ho! If Nobody opens the door, how *can* we walk in?"

"Walk in. And then if Nobody speaks to you, answer him politely, and say your father, one Mr. Maynard, desires his advice and assistance."

"Oh, Father, I do believe you're crazy!" exclaimed Marjorie.

"Never mind," said King, "if Father's crazy, we'll be crazy too! What next, for orders?"

"After that, be guided by your own common sense and good judgment. And,—you wouldn't be frightened at Nobody, would you?"

"No!" declared King. "Nobody could frighten me!"

"Oh, he could, could he? Well, you are a foolish boy if Nobody could frighten you!"

King looked a little confused, and then he laughed and said, "Well, I'd just as lieve fight Nobody, if he attacks me."

"There'll be no cause to fight, my boy. Now, skip along, and remember your message."

"Yes, Mr. Edward Maynard wants advice and assistance from Nobody! Well, I guess that's right, Father, but it all sounds to me like an April Fool joke. Come on, Midget."

As the two children skipped away, King said, thoughtfully, "What does it all mean, Mops?"

"I dunno, King. But it means *something*. It isn't a wild-goose chase, or an April-fool sort of joke. I know Father has some nice surprise for us the way his eyes twinkled."

"Well, but this empty house business seems so silly! I know nobody lives there, for I passed there a few days ago, and it was all shut up."

"Well, we'll soon find out," and the children turned the corner toward the house in question. Sure enough, the blinds were closed and there was no sign of habitation.

"Mr. Nobody lives here, all right!" said King as they entered the gate.

"And such a pretty place, too," commented Marjorie, looking at the luxuriant vines that ran riot over the front veranda.

King rang the bell, feeling half-angry and half-silly at the performance. In a moment the door swung open, but no person was seen.

"Well!" exclaimed King. "Nobody opened that door!"

"We must walk in," said Midget. "Father said so."

"Oh, I hate to! We really haven't any right to go into a strange house like this!"

"But Father said to! Come on!" And grasping King's hand, Midget urged him inside. They stood in the middle of a pretty and attractively furnished hall, but saw or heard no people.

"Hello, Mr. Nobody!" said Marjorie, still clasping King's hand tightly, for the situation was a little weird.

"Hello, yourself!" responded a cheery voice, but they couldn't see any one.

The voice reassured King, and he said, humorously, "I see Nobody! How do you do, sir?"

"Quite well," answered the same voice, but it was a bit muffled, and they couldn't judge where it came from. Also it sounded very gay and laughing, and Marjorie thought it seemed a bit familiar, though she couldn't place it.

"My father sent a message," went on King, sturdily. "He says he wants Nobody's advice and assistance."

"What a self-reliant man!" said the voice, and then from behind a portiere a laughing face appeared, followed by a man's active body. At the same time, from an opposite portiere, a lady sprang out and took Marjorie in her arms.

"Cousin Ethel!"

"Cousin Jack!"

And the children laughed in glee as they recognized Mr. and Mrs. Bryant.

"You dear things!" the lady exclaimed. "I think it's awful to startle you so, but it's the joke of your father and your Cousin Jack. I was afraid it would scare you. Did it?"

"Not exactly," said Marjorie, cuddling in Cousin Ethel's arms, but King protested:

"No, indeed!" he declared. "I wasn't scared, but I felt a little queer."

"You're two Ducky Daddles!" Cousin Ethel cried, and Cousin Jack slapped King on the shoulder and said, "You're a trump, old man!" and King felt very grown-up and manly.

"What's it all about?" he inquired, and Mr. Bryant replied:

"Well, you see, if you've room for us here in Seacote, we're going to stay here for a while. In fact, we've taken this shack with such an intention."

"Oh!" cried Marjorie. "You've taken this house for the summer, and Father knew it, and sent us over here to be surprised!"

"You've sized up the situation exactly, Mehitabel," said Cousin Jack, who loved to call Midget by this old-fashioned name. "And now, if we were properly invited, and very strongly urged, we *might* be persuaded to go home to dinner with you."

"Oh," cried Marjorie, a light breaking in upon her, "you're the dinner guests they're expecting!"

"We sure are!" said Cousin Jack. "And as this is the first time we've been invited out to dinner in Seacote, we're impatient to go."

So they set off for the Maynard house, and Midget led the way with Cousin Ethel.

"When did you come?" she inquired.

"Only this morning, dear. We're not quite set to rights yet, though I brought my own servants, and they'll soon have us all comfy."

"And how did you and Father fix up this plan?"

"He was over here this afternoon, and he and Cousin Jack planned it. Then, as soon as you left your house, your father telephoned over here, and we prepared to receive you in that crazy fashion. Of course, Jack opened the door and stayed behind it. You weren't frightened, were you?"

"No, not really. But it seemed a little,—a little creepy, you know."

"Of course it did!" cried Cousin Jack from behind them. "But that house is so overhung with creepers it makes you feel creepy anyway. I'm going to call it Creeper Castle."

"Oh, don't!" said Marjorie. "It sounds horrid! Makes you think of caterpillars and things like that!"

"So it does! Well, Mehitabel, you name it for us. I can't live in a house without a name."

"I'd call it Bryant Bower. That sounds flowery and pretty."

"Just the ticket! You're a genius for names! Bryant Bower it is. What's the name of your house,—Maynard Mansion?"

"Maynard Manor is prettier," suggested Cousin Ethel.

"So it is! Maynard Manor goes! I don't know anybody with prettier manners than the Maynards, especially the younger generation of them," and though Cousin Jack spoke laughingly, there was an earnest undertone in his voice that greatly pleased King and Marjorie.

"Hooray!" cried that hilarious gentleman, as they reached the Maynards' veranda. "Hello, Ed. How d'ye do, Helen? Here we are! We're returning your youngsters right side up with care. Why, look who's here!" and catching up Rosy Posy, he tossed her high in the air, to the little girl's great delight.

Dinner was a festive occasion indeed, and afterward they all sat on the wide veranda and listened to the roar of the waves.

"This is a restful place," said Cousin Ethel, as she leaned back comfortably in her wicker rocker.

"So it is," agreed her husband, "but, if you ask *me*, I think it's *too* restful. I like a place with some racket to it, don't you, Hezekiah?"

This was his pet name for King, and the boy replied:

"There's fun enough here, Cousin Jack, if you make it yourself."

"That's so, is it? Well, I guess I'll try to make some. Let's see, isn't Fourth of July next week?"

"Yes, it is," said Marjorie. "Next week, Wednesday."

"Well, that's a good day to have fun; and an especially good day for a racket. What shall we do, kiddies?"

"Do you mean for us to choose?" asked Marjorie.

Carolyn Wells

"No, Mehitabel; you suggest, and I'll choose. You think of the very nicest sort of celebrations you know, and I'll select the nicest of them all."

"Well," said Midget, thoughtfully, "there's a party or a picnic. How many people do you mean, Cousin Jack? And do you mean children or grown-ups?"

"Now I feel aggrieved, and insulted, and chagrined, and many other awful things!" Cousin Jack looked so woe-begone that they almost thought him in earnest. "You *know*, Mehitabel, that I'm but a child myself! I'm not a grown-up, and I never will be!"

"That's so!" laughed his wife.

"And so, us children will have a celebration of the children, for the children, and by the children! How many perfectly good children do you know down here?"

"Not many," said King; "hardly any, in fact, except the Sand Club."

"The Sand Club! That sounds interesting. Tell me about it."

So King and Marjorie told all about the Sand Club and its six members, and Cousin Jack declared that was just enough for his idea of a Fourth of July celebration.

"Now for the plan," he went on. "How about a picnic in the woods, which I see sticking up over there, and then come back to Bryant Bower for some fireworks later?"

"I think that sounds beautiful!" said Marjorie, and King entirely agreed.

"Why not have the fireworks here?" said Mr. Maynard. "You're too good to these children, Jack."

"Not a bit of it. We can have a celebration here some other night. But I've picked out the glorious Fourth for my own little racketty-packetty party. You see, on that day we can make all the noise we like and not get arrested."

"Can we dress up, Cousin Jack?" asked Marjorie.

"Sure, child; wear your best bib and tucker, if you like, but I like you better in your play-clothes."

"I don't mean that. I mean costumes."

"Midget is great for dressing up," explained King. "She always wants some cheesecloth wobbed around her, and veils and feathers on her head."

"Oh, I see! Why, yes, I rather guess we *can* dress up."

"I'll wear a red, white, and blue sash, and a liberty cap," said Midget, her eyes dancing.

"Oh, we can do better than that," responded Cousin Jack. "Let's see; we'll make it a sort of reception affair, and you, Mehitabel, can be the Goddess of Liberty, or Miss Columbia, whichever you like. Hezekiah, you can be Uncle Sam! Your respected Cousin Ethel and I will guarantee your costume."

"I want to be a somefin'," spoke up Rosamond, who had been allowed to stay up later than usual, in honor of the guests.

"So you shall, Babykins. I guess we'll let Sister be Miss Columbia, and you shall be a dear little Goddess of Liberty all your own self! How's that?" and Cousin Jack beamed at the smiling Rosy Posy.

"Now, where shall the picnic be?" asked Cousin Ethel, ready to help along the plans.

"There's a lovely grove over beyond the pier," said Midget; "we might go there."

"The very place!" said Cousin Jack; "and we'll have a sand-pail picnic. Didn't you say your coat-of-arms was a sand-pail?"

"Yes, that's the Emblem of the Club."

"And a fine emblem for a picnic. We'll have pails of sandwiches and cakes, and a pail of lemonade, and a pail of ice cream. How's that for emblems?"

"Fine!" said King. "Shall I invite the guests?"

"Yes, my boy. Tell them to assemble here at three o'clock, and we'll depart at once. Tell them all to wear red, white, and blue in honor of the day."

"And do we catch firecrackers?"

"Little ones,—and torpedoes. But no cannon crackers or cap-pistols or bombs or any firearms. I'm not going to have a hospitalful of gunpowder victims on my hands the next day."

"And now," said Mrs. Maynard, "as these wonderful affairs of the nation seem to be all settled, I think you young patriots must skip to bed. Your father and I would like a few words ourselves with these guests of ours."

"Guests of *ours*," corrected Midget, gayly. "Cousin Jack says he's never going to grow up!"

But after lingering good-nights, the brother and sister, arm in arm, went into the house.

"Aren't they dandies!" exclaimed King, as they went upstairs.

"Gay!" agreed Marjorie. "Won't we have fun on the Fourth! Oh, I was *so* surprised to see them, weren't you, King?"

"Yep. The Craigs will like Cousin Jack, won't they?"

"Yes, indeed, and Hester, too. Good-night, King."

"Good-night, Mopsy Midget. Here!" and as a final compliment, King pulled off her hair-ribbon and handed it to her with a dancing-school bow.

Marjorie gave his hair an affectionate tweak, and with these good-natured attentions they parted.

CHAPTER VII

THE GLORIOUS FOURTH

The sun rose early on Fourth of July morning. For he knew many patriotic young hearts were beating with impatience for the great day to begin. Moreover, he rose clear and bright, and yet he didn't shine down too hotly for the comfort of those same young people. In fact, it was a perfect summer day.

Marjorie sprang out of bed and began to dress, with glad anticipations. The Bryants were to spend the day at Maynard Manor, until time for the afternoon picnic, and after the picnic came the reception at Bryant Bower.

Midget put on a fresh white pique, and tied up her mop of curls with wide bows of red, white, and blue ribbon.

When all ready she went dancing downstairs, pausing on her way to tap at King's door.

"All ready, Kinksie?" she called out.

"In a minute, Mops. Wait for me!"

Midget sat down on the staircase window-seat, and in a moment King joined her there.

"Hello, Mopsy-Doodle! Merry Fourth of Ju—New Year's!"

"Hello, yourself! Oh, King, isn't it a gorgeous day? What shall we do first?"

"I dunno! We can't shoot things or make much noise, until Father and Mother get up. It would be mean to wake them."

"Oh, pshaw! they can't be asleep through all this racket that is going on. Hear the shooting all around."

"Well, we'll see. Let's get outdoors, anyhow."

The children opened the front door, and there, sitting on the veranda steps, his head leaning against a pillar, sat Cousin Jack, apparently sound asleep.

"Will you look at that!" said King, in a whisper. "Has he been here all night, do you s'pose?"

"No, 'course not. But I s'pose he's been here some time. Do you think he's really asleep?"

"He looks so. What shall we do with him?"

"Dress him up," commanded Marjorie, promptly, and pulling off her wide hair-ribbons, she proceeded to tie one around Cousin Jack's neck, and one around his head, giving that gentleman a very festive appearance.

After she had arranged the bows to her satisfaction, Cousin Jack obligingly woke up,—though, as a matter of fact, he hadn't been to sleep!

"Why, if here isn't Mehitabel!" he exclaimed; "and Hezekiah, too! What a surprise!"

"How do you like your decorations?" asked Marjorie, surveying him with admiration.

"Oh, are these ribbons *real*? I thought I was dreaming, and had a Fourth of July nightmare."

"How long have you been here, Cousin Jack?" asked King.

"Well, I was waking, so I called early; I don't know at what hour, but I've been long enough alone, so I'm glad you two young patriots came down to help me celebrate. Polly want a firecracker?" He held out a pack of small ones to Marjorie, but she declined them.

"No, thank you; give those to King. I'd rather have torpedoes."

"All right, my girlie, here you are! And here's a cap to replace the ribbons you so kindly gave me."

Cousin Jack drew from his pocket a tissue-paper cap, that had evidently come in a snapping-cracker. Then he produced another one for King, and one which he laid aside for Rosy Posy. They were gay red, white, and blue caps, with cockades and streamers.

"Now, we'll be a procession," he went on. From a nook on the veranda, where he had hidden them, he produced a drum, a tambourine, and a cornet.

The cornet was his own, and he presented the drum to King, and the tambourine to Marjorie.

"Form in line!" he ordered; "forward,—march!"

He led the line, and the two children followed.

Being a good cornet player, Cousin Jack made fine martial music, and King and Midget had sufficient sense of rhythm to accompany him on the drum and tambourine. After marching round the house once, Cousin Jack went up the steps and in at the front door. Upstairs and through the halls, and down again.

Nurse Nannie and Rosamond appeared at the nursery door, and were instructed to fall in line behind the others. Then Sarah, the waitress, was discovered, looking on from the dining-room, and she, too, was told to march.

At last Mr. and Mrs. Maynard appeared, laughing at this invasion of their morning nap.

They sat in state in the veranda-chairs, as on a reviewing-stand, while the grand parade marched and countermarched on the lawn in front of them.

"All over!" cried Cousin Jack, at last. "Break ranks!"

The company dispersed, and Sarah returned, giggling, to her duties.

"Such a foine man as Misther Bryant do be!" she said to the cook. "Shure, he's just like wan of the childher."

And so he was. Full of patriotic enthusiasm, Cousin Jack set off bombs and firecrackers, until the elder Maynards declared that their ears ached, and the roisterers must come in to breakfast.

"I must go home," announced their guest. "I have a wife and six small children dependent on me for support."

As a matter of fact, the Bryants had no children, and Mrs. Maynard declared she should telephone for Cousin Ethel to come to breakfast, too, so Cousin Jack consented to stay.

The breakfast party was an unexpected addition to the day's festivities, but Mrs. Maynard was equal to the occasion. She scurried around and found flags to decorate the table, and tied a red, white, and blue balloon to the back of each chair, which gave the room a gay appearance.

The vigorous exercise had produced good appetites, and full

justice was done to Ellen's creamed chicken and hot rolls and coffee.

"Who's for a dip in the ocean?" asked Cousin Jack, when breakfast was over.

All were included in this pleasing suggestion, and soon a bathing-suited party threw themselves into the dashing whitecaps.

Cousin Jack tried to teach Marjorie to swim, but it is not easy to learn to swim in the surf, and she made no very great progress. But Mr. Maynard and Mr. Bryant swam out to a good distance, and King was allowed to accompany them, as he already was a fair swimmer.

Marjorie held fast to the rope, and jumped about, now almost carried away by a big wave, and now thrown back toward the beach by another.

It was rather rough bathing, so the ladies of the party and Midget left the water before the others.

"*Aren't* we having fun!" exclaimed Marjorie, as she trudged, dripping, through the sand, to the bath-house. "Oh, Cousin Ethel, I'm *so* glad you came down here."

"I'm glad, too, dear. I believe Jack enjoys you children more than he does any of his friends of his own age."

"Jack's just like a boy," said Mrs. Maynard, "and I think he always will be. He's like Peter Pan,—never going to grow up."

And it did seem so. After the bath, Mr. Bryant marched the children down to the pier for ice cream.

Mrs. Maynard remonstrated a little, but she was informed that Fourth of July only came once a year, and extra indulgences were in order.

So King and Midget and Cousin Jack went gayly along the long pier that ran far out into the ocean. On either side were booths where trinkets and seaside souvenirs were sold, and Cousin Jack bought a shell necklace for Midget, and a shell watch-fob for King.

Then he ordered a dozen little tin pails sent to his own house.

"For my picnic," he explained, as Midget looked at him wonderingly. "It's to be a sand-pail picnic, you know."

As they neared the ice-cream garden, Marjorie noticed a forlorn-looking little boy, near the entrance. So wistful did he look, that she turned around to look at him again.

"Who's your friend, Mehitabel?" said Mr. Bryant, seeing her glance.

"Oh, I don't know, Cousin Jack!" she cried, impulsively; "but he seems so poor and lonesome, and we're all so happy. Couldn't I go without my ice cream, and let him have it? Oh, please let me!"

"H'm! he isn't a very attractive specimen of humanity."

"Well, he isn't very clean, but, see, he has a nice face, and big brown eyes! Oh, do give him some ice cream, Cousin Jack; I'll willingly go without."

"I'll go without," said King, quickly; "you can have mine, Mops."

Cousin Jack looked quizzically at the children.

"I might say I'd give you each ice cream, and the poor kiddie also. But that would be my charity. Now, if you two really want to do the poor little chap a kindness, you may each have a half portion, and give him a whole plate. How's that?"

"Fine!" exclaimed Marjorie; "just the thing! But, truly, Cousin Jack, it isn't *much* sacrifice for us, for we'll have ice cream at the picnic, anyhow."

"That's right, girlie; don't claim any more credit than belongs to you. Well, next thing is to invite your young friend."

So Marjorie went over to the poor little boy, and said, kindly:

"It's Fourth of July, and we'd like you to come and eat ice cream with us."

The child's face brightened up, but immediately a look of distrust came into his eyes, and he said:

"Say, is youse kiddin' me?"

"No," said King, for Marjorie didn't know quite what he meant; "we mean it. We're going to have ice cream, and we want you to have some with us."

"Kin I bring me brudder?"

"Where is he?" asked Cousin Jack, smiling at this new development of the case.

"Over dere, wit' me sister. Kin I bring 'em both?"

Marjorie laughed outright at this, but Mr. Bryant said, gravely:

"How many in your entire family? Let me know the worst at once!"

"Dat's all; me brudder an' sister. Kin they come, too?"

"Yes, if they're fairly clean," and the boy ran to get them. He came back bringing a boy but little smaller than himself, and a tiny girl.

Though not immaculate, they were presentable, and soon the six were seated at a round table.

Cousin Jack conformed to his decree that the Maynard children should have but a half-portion each, but he added that this was partly due to his consideration for their health, as well as his willingness that the charity should be partly theirs. But he told his three guests that they could eat as much as they chose; and noting their generally hungry appearance, he ordered a first course of sandwiches for them, which kindness was greatly appreciated.

"Gee! Youse is a white man!" exclaimed the oldest visitor, as he scraped his saucer almost through its enamel.

"What does he mean?" asked Midget, laughing. "Of course, you're a white man."

"That's slang, Marjorie, for a desirable citizen."

"Funny sort of slang," Midget commented; "a white man is plain English, isn't it?"

"I mean, he's white clear through," volunteered the boy, whose quick eyes darted from one face to another of his benefactors.

"Yes, I can understand that," said Midget, slowly; "it just means you're good all through, Cousin Jack, and I quite agree to that."

After the small visitors' hunger was entirely appeased, Cousin Jack presented them each with a flag and a packet of torpedoes, and sent them away rejoicing.

"Poor little scraps of humanity," he said; "I hope, Mehitabel, you'll always bring a little sunshine into such lives when opportunity presents itself."

"I will, Cousin Jack. Are they very poor?"

"No, not so very. But they never have any fun, or anything very good to eat. Of course, you can't be an organized charity, but once in a while, if you can make a poor child happy by the expenditure of a small sum, do it."

"We will," cried King, impressed by Cousin Jack's earnestness. "But we don't have much money to spend, you know."

"You have an allowance, don't you?"

"Yes; we each have fifty cents a week, Mops and Kitty and I."

"Well, Kitty isn't here, so I can't ask her; but I'm going to ask you two dear friends of mine, to give away one-tenth of your income to charity. Now, how much would that be?"

"Five cents a week," replied Marjorie.

"Well, will you do it? Every week give a nickel, or a nickel's worth of peanuts or lemonade or something to some poor little kiddie who doesn't have much fun in life? And you needn't do it every week, if it isn't convenient, but lay aside the nickel each week, and then give a larger sum, as it accumulates."

"Sure we will, Cousin Jack," said King, and Midget said, "Yes, indeed! I'll be glad to. We can most always catch a poor child, somewhere."

"Well, if not, just save it up till you do. You'll find plenty of opportunities in the winter, in Rockwell, I'm sure."

"Yes, sir-ee!" said Midget, remembering the poor family whose house burned down not long ago. "And I'm glad you advised us about this, Cousin Jack. I'm going to ask the Craig boys and Hester to do it, too."

"Better be careful, Mehitabel. I can advise you, because we're good chums, and I'm a little older than you, though I don't look it! But I'm not sure you ought to take the responsibility of advising your young friends. You might suggest it to them, —merely suggest it, you know, and if their agree and their parents agree, why, then, all right. And now home to our own luncheon. I declare it made me hungry to see those children eat!"

Promptly at three o'clock that afternoon the Sand Club gathered for the Sand-Pail Picnic. By making two trips the Maynards' big motor carried them all to the picnic grove, about a mile distant.

Here Cousin Jack provided all sorts of sports for them. At a target, they shot with bows and arrows, and the boys were allowed a little rifle-shooting.

There was that funny game of picking up potatoes with teaspoons, followed by a rollicking romp at Blindman's Buff. Then Cousin Jack marshalled his young friends into line, and they all sang "Star-Spangled Banner," and "Columbia," and "America," and cheered, and fired off mild explosives, and had a real Fourth of July celebration. Then the feast was brought on.

The children sat cross-legged on the grass, and each one was given a tin sand-pail.

But instead of sand, the pail was found to contain sandwiches and crisp little cakes known as sand-tarts.

After these there were served dainty little paper pails, from a caterer's, filled with ice cream.

"What a lovely sand picnic!" exclaimed Marjorie, as she sat on the sand, blissfully disposing of her ice cream. "I'm going to call Cousin Jack, The Sandman!"

"Ho! a Sandman puts you to sleep!" cried Tom Craig; "let's get a better name than that for Mr. Bryant."

Carolyn Wells

"Call him Sandy Claus," piped up Dick, and they all laughed.

"A little out of season, but it's all right, my boy," said Cousin Jack. "Call me anything you like, as long as you call me early and often. Now, shall we be trotting home again, to continue our revels?"

With a sigh of utter content, Marjorie climbed into the motor, and they went spinning home to dress for the "Reception."

At the reception more guests were invited, and Bryant Bower quite justified its pretty name.

Japanese lanterns dotted the grounds, and hung among the vines of the veranda. Flags and bunting were everywhere, and a small platform, draped with red, white, and blue, had been erected for the receiving party.

This consisted of King, Midget, and Rosy Posy in patriotic costume.

King, as Uncle Sam, presented a funny figure with his white beaver hat, his long-tailed blue coat, and red and white striped trousers. Midget wore a becoming "Miss Columbia" costume, with a liberty cap and liberty pole and flag. Rosamond was a chubby little Goddess of Liberty, but she preferred to run around everywhere, rather than stand still and receive.

King and Midget did the honors gracefully, and after all the guests had assembled, they took seats on the lawn to watch the fireworks.

These were of a fine quality, and as the flowerpots and bombs burst into stars in the sky both children and grown-ups joined in loud applause.

There was patriotic music, and more ice cream, and when, at last, it was all over, the Sand Club went together to thank Cousin Jack for the entertainment.

"Glad you liked it," he said, heartily; "and now, scamper home and to bed, all of you, so your parents won't say I made you lose your beauty sleep."

CHAPTER VIII

A REVELATION

Marjorie was practising.

It was a lovely afternoon, and she wanted to go out and play, but her hour's practising must be done first. She was conscientious about it, and tried very hard to hold her hands just right, as she counted, one—two—three—four; one—two—three—four.

Mrs. Corey, Hester's mother, was calling on Mrs. Maynard, and the two ladies sat on the veranda, just outside the window near which the piano stood.

Marjorie did not listen to their conversation, for it was of no interest to her, and, too, she was devoting all her attention to her exercises. Usually, she didn't mind practising, but to-day the Sand Club was waiting for her, and her practice hour seemed interminable.

"One—two—three—four," she counted to herself, when something Mrs. Corey said arrested her attention.

"Your oldest daughter?" Marjorie heard her exclaim; "you amaze me!"

Midget had no thought of eavesdropping, and as the piano was near the open window, surely they could hear her practising, and so knew she was there.

But Mrs. Maynard answered, in a low, serious voice, "Yes, my oldest girl. She is not our child. She is a foundling. We adopted her when an infant."

"Really?" said Mrs. Corey, much interested. "How did that happen?"

"Well," said Mrs. Maynard, "my husband desired it, and I consented. She has grown up a good girl, but of course I can't feel toward her as I feel toward my own children."

"No, of course not," agreed Mrs. Corey. "The others are all your own?"

"Yes, they are my own."

"She doesn't know this, does she?"

"Oh, no, we have never let her suspect it. She thinks I am her mother, and she thinks I love her as I do my own children. But it is hard for me to pretend affection for her, when I remember her humble origin."

"Your husband? Does he care for her?"

"He feels much as I do. You see, she is not of as fine a nature as our own children. Of course he can't help seeing that. But we both do our best for the girl."

"Good for you, Mrs. Maynard; that's fine!"

"Do you really think so, Mrs. Corey? I'm afraid that—"

But Marjorie heard no more. She had stopped her practising at the first words of these awful disclosures.

Not her mother's own child! She, Marjorie Maynard! It

couldn't be possible! But as the conversation went on, perfectly audible, though not in loud tones, she could no longer doubt the truth of what her mother was saying.

Dreadful it might be,—unbelievable it might be,—but true it must be.

"One—two—three—four," mechanically she tried to strike the keys, but her fingers refused to move.

She left the piano, and went slowly up to her own room.

Her pretty room that her mother,—no, that Mrs. Maynard,— had fixed up for her with flowering chintz hangings and frilly white curtains.

Not her mother! Who, then, was or had been her mother?

And then Marjorie's calm gave way. She threw herself on her little white bed, and burying her face in the pillow she sobbed convulsively. Her thoughts flew to her father,—but no, he wasn't her father! King wasn't her brother,—nor Kitty her sister! Nor Rosy Posy—?

It was all too dreadful. At every fresh thought about it, it grew worse. Dear old King, she had never realized before how much she loved him. And Kitty! And Father and Mother! She *would* call them that, even though they were no relation to her.

For a long time Marjorie cried,—great, deep, heart-racking sobs that wore her out.

At last she settled down into a calm of despair.

"I am going away," she said, to herself. "I won't stay here where they have to *pretend* they love me! Oh, Mother, *Mother*!"

But no one heard the little girl's grief. Mrs. Maynard still sat on the veranda, talking to Mrs. Corey; King was down at Sand Court; and the nurse had taken Rosamond out for a walk.

"I *must* go away," poor Marjorie went on; "I *can't* stay here, I should *suffocate*!"

She sat up on the edge of her bed, and clasped her hands in utter desolation. Where could she go? Not to Cousin Ethel's, she'd only bring her back home. *Home!* She hadn't any home,—no *real* home! She thought of Grandma Sherwood's, but she wasn't her grandma at all! Then she thought of Grandma Maynard. That was a curious thought, for though Grandma Maynard wasn't her own grandmother, either, yet, a few months ago, she had begged Marjorie to live with her and be her little girl. Surely she must have *known* that Midget wasn't really her granddaughter, and yet she had really loved her enough to want her to live there.

Then Grandma Maynard wouldn't have to *pretend* to love her.

Clearly, that was the only thing to do. She couldn't run away, with no destination in view.

She had no claim on Grandma Sherwood or Uncle Steve, but Grandma Maynard *had* wanted her,—really *wanted* her.

Marjorie looked at the little clock on her dressing table. It was almost three o'clock. She knew there was a train to New York about three, and she resolved to go on it.

At first she thought of taking some things in a bag, but she decided not to, as she didn't want any of the things the Maynards had given her.

"Oh," she thought, while the tears came afresh; "my name isn't even Maynard! I don't know *what* it is!"

She put on a blue linen dress, and a blue hat with roses on it. Some instinct of sadness made her tie her hair with

Carolyn Wells

black ribbon.

As she went downstairs, she heard Mrs. Corey say, "I am astounded at these revelations!" and her mother replied, "Dear friend, I knew you would be."

Marjorie wasn't crying then, she felt as if she had no tears left. She shut her teeth together hard, and went out by a side door. This way she could reach the street unobserved, and she walked straight ahead to the railroad station. She had a five-dollar gold piece that Uncle Steve had sent her on Christmas, and that, with a little silver change, she carried in her pocketbook. But she left behind her pearl ring and all the little trinkets or valuables she possessed.

She felt as if her heart had turned to stone. It wasn't so much anger at Mr. and Mrs. Maynard as it was that awful sense of desolation,—as if the world had come to an end.

At one moment she would think she missed King the most; then with the thought of her father, a rush of tears would come; and then her poor little tortured heart would cry out, "Oh, Mother, *Mother!*"

She knew perfectly well the way to New York, and though the station agent looked at her sharply when she bought a ticket, he said nothing. For Marjorie was a self-possessed little girl, of good manners and quiet air when she chose to be. With her ticket in her hand, she sat down to wait for the train. There were few people in the station at that hour, and no one who knew her.

When the train came puffing in, she went out and took it, in a matter-of-fact way, as if quite accustomed to travelling alone.

Really, she felt very much frightened. She had never been on a train alone before, and the noise of the cars and the bustle of the people, and the shouting of the trainmen made her nervous.

And then, with a fresh flood of woe, the remembrance of *why* she was going would come over her, and obliterate all other considerations.

For perhaps half an hour she kept the tears back bravely enough; but as she rode on, and realized more and more deeply what it all meant, she could control herself no longer, and burst into a paroxysm of weeping.

She was sitting next the window, and, as there were few passengers, no one was in the seat with her.

But when she raised her head, exhausted by her outburst of tears, a burly red-faced man sat beside her.

"Come, come, little one, what's it all about?" he said.

His tone was kind, but his personality was not pleasant, and Marjorie felt no inclination to confide in him.

"Nothing, sir," she said, drawing as far away from him as possible.

"Now, now, little miss, you can't cry like that, and then say there's nothing the matter."

Marjorie wanted to rebuke his intrusion, but she didn't know exactly what to say, so she turned toward the window and resolutely kept looking out.

The trees and fields flying by were not very comforting. Every mile took her farther away from her dear ones, for they *were* dear, whether related to her or not.

She pressed her flushed cheeks against the cool window pane. She was too exhausted to cry any more. She seemed to have only enough strength to say, brokenly, "Oh, Mother, *Mother!*" and then from sheer weariness of flesh she fell into a troubled sleep.

Meantime Marjorie was missed at home. The Sand Club grew tired of waiting for her, and King went up to the house to investigate the delay.

He trudged, whistling, up the driveway, and seeing Mrs. Corey, he whipped off his cap, and greeted her politely.

"Where's Midget, Mother?" he asked.

"I don't know, son; isn't she with you?"

"No'm, and I'm tired waiting for her."

"Is Hester there?" asked Mrs. Corey.

"Yes, Mrs. Corey, Hester's been with us an hour, and we're waiting for Mopsy. She said she'd come as soon as she finished her practising."

"She stopped practising some time ago," said Mrs. Corey. "I haven't heard the piano for half an hour or more."

"I'll bet she's tucked away somewhere, reading!" exclaimed King; "I'll hunt her out!"

"Perhaps she's gone over to Cousin Ethel's," suggested Mrs. Maynard.

"I'll hunt her up," repeated King, and he went into the house.

"Marjorie Mops! I say! Come out of that!" he cried, banging at the closed door of her bedroom.

Getting no reply, he opened the door and looked in, but she wasn't there.

"You old scallywag Mops!" he cried, shaking his fist at her empty room, "I never knew you to go back on your word before! And you said you'd come to Sand Court as soon as you could!"

He looked in the veranda hammock, and in the library, and any place where he thought Midget might be, absorbed in a book; he inquired of the servants; and at last he went back to his mother.

"I can't find Mopsy," he said.

"Then she *must* be over at Cousin Ethel's. She does love to go over there."

"Well, she oughtn't to go when she's promised to come out with us. I never knew old Midge to break a promise before."

"Perhaps Cousin Ethel telephoned for her," suggested Mrs. Maynard. "Though in that case, she should have told me she was going. Run over there and see, son."

"I'll telephone over, that'll be quicker," said King, and ran back into the house.

"Nope," he said, returning; "she isn't there, and hasn't been there to-day. Mother, don't you think it's queer?"

"Why, yes, King, it is a little queer. But she can't be far away. Perhaps she walked down to the train to meet Father."

"Oh, Mother, that would be a crazy thing to do, when she knew we were waiting for her."

"Well, maybe she went walking with Rosamond and Nurse Nannie. She's certainly somewhere around. Run away now, King. Mrs. Corey and I are busy."

King walked slowly away.

"It's pretty queer," he said to Hester and the Craig boys; "Mops is nowhere to be found."

Carolyn Wells

"Well, don't look so scared," said Tom; "she can't be kidnapped. If it was your baby sister, that would be different. But Midget has just gone off on some wild-goose chase,—or she is hiding to tease us."

"Perhaps she wrote to Kitty," suggested Hester, "and went down to the post-office to mail it."

"Not likely," said King. "She knows the postman collects at six o'clock. Well, I s'pose she *is* hiding somewhere, reading a book. Won't I give it to her when I catch her! For she *said* she'd come out here, right after her practice hour."

A dullness seemed to fall on the Sand Club members present. Not only was Marjorie their ringleader and moving spirit, but somehow King's uneasiness impressed all of them, and soon Dick Craig said, "I'm going home."

King raised no objection, and, after sitting listlessly around for a few moments, the others all went home.

But Tom turned back.

"I say," he began, "you know Mopsy is somewhere, all right."

"Of course she's somewhere, Tom, but she never did anything like this before, and I can't understand it. The only thing I can think of is, that she's gone down on the pier. But she never goes there alone."

"Well, there's lots of things she might be doing. Come on, let's go down on the pier and take a look."

The two boys walked out to the end of the pier and back again, but saw no sign of Marjorie.

On their way home, Tom turned in at his own house.

"Good-by, old chap," he said; "don't look so worried. Midget will be sitting up laughing at you when you get home."

King said good-by, and went on. He felt a strange depression of heart, as if something must have happened to Midget. He knew his mother felt no alarm, and perhaps it was foolish, but the fact remained that Midge had never acted like that before. Mr. Maynard came home at six o'clock, and Marjorie had not yet made an appearance.

He looked very much alarmed, and at sight of his anxiety, Mrs. Maynard grew worried.

"Why, Ed," she exclaimed, "you don't think there's anything wrong, do you?"

"I hope not, Helen, but it's so unusual. I can only think of the ocean. Does she ever go down and sit on the beach alone?"

"No," said King, positively; "she never does anything like that, alone. We're always together."

"And you hadn't had any quarrel, or anything?"

"Oh, no, Father; nothing of the sort. She went to practise right after luncheon, and said she'd be out in an hour."

"I heard her practising, while Mrs. Corey was here," said Mrs. Maynard, reminiscently; "but I don't remember just when she stopped."

"Well," said Mr. Maynard, "it's extraordinary, but I can't think anything's wrong with the child. You know she always has been mischievous, and I think she's playing some game on us. We may as well go to dinner."

But nobody could eat dinner. The sight of Midget's empty chair began to seem tragic, and King choked and left the table.

Mrs. Maynard burst into tears, and rose also. Her husband

followed her.

"Don't worry, Helen," he urged; "she's sure to be safe and sound somewhere."

"Oh, I don't know, Ed! Such a thing as this never happened before! Oh, find her, Ed, *do* find her!"

King had run over to the Bryants' and now returned, accompanied by those two very much alarmed people.

"We must *do* something!" exclaimed Cousin Jack. "Of course something has happened to the child! She isn't one to cut up any such game on purpose. Have you looked in her room?"

"What for?" asked Mrs. Maynard, helplessly.

"Why, to see if you can discover anything unusual. I'm going up!"

Mr. Bryant flew upstairs two steps at a time, and they all followed. But nothing unusual was to be seen. The pretty room was in order, and no clothing of any sort was lying about.

Mrs. Maynard looked in the cupboard.

"Why, her blue linen is gone!" she said, "and here's the white pique she had on at luncheon. And her blue hat is gone; she must have dressed up to go out somewhere to call, and unexpectedly stayed to dinner."

"Does she ever do that?" demanded Cousin Jack.

"She never has before," answered Mrs. Maynard, falling weakly back on Marjorie's bed. "Why, this pillow is all wet!"

They looked at each other in consternation. They saw, too, the deep imprint of a head in the dented pillow. Surely, this meant tragedy of some sort, for if the child had sobbed so hard, she must have been in deep trouble.

"We must find her!" said Cousin Jack, starting for the stairs.

Carolyn Wells

CHAPTER IX

THE SEARCH

It was fortunate that the Bryants were there to take the initiative, for Mr. and Mrs. Maynard seemed incapable of action. Usually alert and energetic, they were so stunned at the thought of real disaster to Marjorie that they sat around helplessly inactive.

"Come with me, King," said Cousin Jack, going to the telephone in the library.

Then he called up every house in Seacote where Marjorie could possibly have gone, and King helped by suggesting the names of acquaintances.

But no one could give any news of the little girl; no one whom they asked had seen or heard of her that afternoon.

Cousin Jack's face grew very white, and his features were drawn, as he said: "You stay here, Ed, with Helen and Ethel; King and I will go out for a bit. Come, King."

Kingdon said nothing; he snatched up his cap and went along silently by Mr. Bryant's side, trying to keep up with his companion's long, swift strides.

To the beach they went; it was not yet quite dark, but of course they saw no sign of Marjorie.

"Are you thinking she might have been washed away by the waves?" asked King, in a quivering voice.

"That's all I *can* think of," replied Mr. Bryant, grimly.

"But it isn't likely, Cousin Jack. Mopsy is really a heavyweight, you know. And there's not a very big surf on now."

"That's so, King. But where *can* she be?" Then they went and talked with the fishermen, and then on to the Life-saving Station.

The big, good-hearted men all knew Marjorie, and all declared she had not been on the beach that afternoon,—at least, not within their particular locality.

Discouraged, Cousin Jack and King turned down toward the pier. Their inquiries were fruitless; though many people knew Midget, by sight, none had seen her. There was nothing to do but go back home.

"Have you found her?" cried Cousin Ethel, as they entered the house.

"No; but the beach people haven't seen her, so I'm sure there's no accident of that sort." Cousin Jack wouldn't make use of the word drowning, but they all knew what he meant.

Mrs. Maynard sat staring, in a sort of dull apathy. She couldn't realize that Marjorie was lost, she couldn't believe an accident had befallen her, yet, where was she?

"Let's search the house," she said, jumping up suddenly. "I *must* do *something*. Couldn't she have gone somewhere to read quietly, and fallen asleep?"

This was a possibility, and the house was searched from top to bottom by eager hunters. But no Marjorie was found.

Carolyn Wells

As it neared midnight, the ladies were persuaded to go to bed.

"You can do nothing, dear, by remaining up," said Mr. Maynard to his wife. "The Bryants will stay with us to-night, so you and Ethel go to your rooms, and King, too. Jack and I will stay here in the library for a while."

King demurred at being sent away, but his father explained that if he wanted to help, all he could do was to obey orders. So King went upstairs, but not to his own room. About an hour later he came down again, to find his father and Mr. Bryant still sitting in the library waiting for morning.

"Father," said King, his eyes shining bright beneath his tousled hair, "I've been rummaging in Midget's room. I thought I might find out something to help us. And she's taken her pocketbook, and the gold piece Uncle Steve gave her last Christmas. I know, because I know where she always kept it,— and it's gone."

"Well, King," said his father, thoughtfully, "what do you make out from that?"

"Only that she has gone somewhere especial. I mean somewhere to spend that money,—not just for a walk on the beach, or down to the pier."

"That's encouraging," said Cousin Jack, "for if she went away on some special errand, she's more likely to be safe and sound, somewhere. Did you notice anything else missing, King?"

"Not a thing. And you know how wet her pillow was. Well, I think she heard about some poor person or poor family, and she cried about them, and then she took her gold piece and went to help them."

"That's ingenious, King," said Mr. Maynard, "and it may be true. I hope so, I'm sure. But why should she stay away so long and not let us know?"

"Well, you see, the poor family may live at some distance, and not have any telephone, and they may be ill, or something, and she may be there yet, helping. You know Mopsy is awful kind-hearted. Remember the Simpsons' fire? She forgot everything else in caring for them."

"That's so, my son; at any rate, it's the most comforting theory we've had yet, and I'll go and tell your mother about it. It will help her, I know."

Mr. Maynard went away, and King remained downstairs.

"I'm not going to bed, Cousin Jack," he said; "I'm old enough now to stay up with you men, in trouble like this."

"All right, King. You're showing manly traits, my boy, and I'm proud of you. Now, old chap, between you and me, I don't subscribe to your poor-family theory. It's possible, of course, but it doesn't seem probable to me."

"Well, then, Cousin Jack, what can we do next?"

"We can't do anything till morning; then I think we must see the police."

"Oh, that seems so awful!"

"I know, but if it's the means of finding Marjorie?"

"Then, of course, we'll do it! How early can we see them?"

"We can telephone as early as we like, I suppose. But I've little confidence in the powers of the police down here. They're all right to patrol the beach, but they're not like city policemen."

At last the night wore away, and daybreak came.

They telephoned the police, and in a few minutes two of them arrived at the Maynard house for consultation.

"I know the child well," said one of them, "I often see her about,—a well-behaved little lady, but full o' fun, too. D'ye think she might have been kidnapped, now?"

"It might be," said Mr. Bryant, "though she's pretty big for that. And, too, she took extra money with her."

"Then she may have been goin' somewhere by rail."

"That's so! I never thought of that!" and Cousin Jack almost smiled.

"But where would she go?" said Mr. Maynard, hopelessly. "She never travelled alone, and though impulsively mischievous, sometimes, she wouldn't deliberately run away."

The policemen went away to begin their quest, and the Maynards and their guests went to breakfast.

No one felt like eating, yet each urged the others to do so.

"Where's Middy?" inquired baby Rosamond, at table. "Middy gone 'way?"

"Yes, dear," said Cousin Jack, for no one else could speak. "Middy's gone away for a little while."

"I know," said the child, contentedly, "Middy gone to Gramma's to see Kitty!"

"Why, perhaps she did!" exclaimed Mr. Maynard.

But Mrs. Maynard had no such hope. It was too unlike Marjorie to do such a thing.

"Well, let's find out," urged King. "Let's get Uncle Steve on the long-distance wire."

"Don't alarm Grandma," said Mrs. Maynard. "There's no use

stirring her up, until we know ourselves what has happened."

"Leave it to me," said Cousin Jack. "I'll find out."

After some delay, he succeeded in getting Uncle Steve on the telephone. Then he asked for Kitty.

"Hello, Susannah!" he cried, assuming a merry voice, in his kind desire not to alarm her. "This is your Cousin Jack!"

"Oh, hello, Cousin Jack!" exclaimed Kitty, in delight. "How nice of you to call me up! How is everybody?"

"We're well, thank you! How are you all?"

"Oh, we're all right."

"Are you lonesome, away from your family?"

"No, not lonesome, though I'd like to see them. Tell Midget there are two hundred incubator chicks now."

"Well, that *is* a lot! Now, good-by, Kitsie; I can't run up too big a telephone bill for your father. We all send love. Be a good girl. Good-by."

Cousin Jack hung up the receiver and buried his face in his hands. It had been a great strain on his nerves to appear gay and carefree to Kitty, and the implied assurance that Marjorie was *not* there nearly made him give way.

"She isn't there," he said, dully, as he repeated to the family what Kitty had said. And then the telephone rang, and it was the police department.

Mr. Maynard took the receiver.

"We've traced her," came the news, and the father's face grew white with suspense. "She bought a ticket to New York, and went there on the three-o'clock train yesterday afternoon. Nothing further is known, as yet, but as soon as we can get in touch with the conductor of that train, we will."

"New York! Impossible!" cried Cousin Ethel, when she heard the message, and Mrs. Maynard fainted away.

Marjorie! on a train, going to New York alone!

"Come on, King," said Cousin Jack, abruptly, and leaving the others to care for Mrs. Maynard, these two strode off again. Straight to the railroad station they went to interview the agent themselves.

He corroborated the story. He did not know Marjorie's name, but he described the child so exactly that there was no room for doubt of her identity.

But he could tell them no more. She had bought her ticket and taken the train in a quiet, matter-of-fact way, as any passenger would do.

"Did she look as if she had been crying?" asked King, almost crying himself.

"Why, yes, now you speak of it, her face *did* look so. Her eyes was red, and she looked sorter sad. But she didn't say nothin', 'cept to ask for a ticket to New York."

"Return ticket?" put in Mr. Bryant.

"No, sir; a single ticket. Just one way."

The conductor couldn't be seen until afternoon, as his run was a long one, and his home far away.

"I can't understand it," said King, as they walked homeward; "and I can't believe it. If Midget went to New York alone, she had lost her mind,—that's all."

But when they reached home, they found the Maynards quite hopeful. It had occurred to them that, by some strange freak, Marjorie had decided to visit Grandma Maynard, and had started off there alone.

"I'm trying to get them on the long-distance," Mr. Maynard announced, quite cheerily, as they entered.

"Let me take it," said Cousin Jack. "If she *isn't* there, we don't want to alarm them, either."

"That's so!" said Mr. Maynard. "All right, Jack, take it. Bless you, old fellow, for your help."

But when connection had been made, and Cousin Jack found himself in communication with Grandma Maynard, he didn't know what to say. He caught at the first pretext he could think of, and said:

"How do you do, Mrs. Maynard? You don't know me, but I'm Jack Bryant, a guest at Ed Maynard's house in Seacote. Now, won't you tell me when Marjorie's birthday comes?"

"Ah, I've heard of you, Mr. Bryant," said Grandma Maynard, pleasantly. "I suppose you want to surprise the child with a present or a party. Well, her birthday is next week,—the fifteenth of July."

"Oh, thank you. She is getting a big girl, isn't she? When, —when did you see her last?"

Cousin Jack's voice faltered, but the unsuspecting lady, listening, didn't notice it.

"About two months ago. They were here in May. I love Marjorie, and I wish I could see her again, but there's little hope of it. She wrote to me last week that they would be in Seacote all summer."

"Yes, that is their plan," said Cousin Jack.

He could say no more, and dropped the receiver without even a good-by.

But though Grandma Maynard might think him rude or uncourteous, she could not feel frightened or alarmed for Marjorie's safety, because of anything he had said.

"She isn't there," he said, quietly; "but I still think she started for there, and now we have a direction in which to look."

But what a direction! Marjorie, alone, going to New York, endeavoring to find Grandma Maynard's house, and not getting there! Where had she been all night? Where was she now?

There were no answers to these questions. And now Mr. Maynard took the helm. He cast off the apathy that had seemed to paralyze him, and, rising, he began to talk quickly.

"Helen," he said, "try to rouse yourself, darling. Keep up a good hope, and be brave, as you have always been. King, I am going out to find Marjorie. You cannot go with me, for I want to leave your mother in your care. You have proved yourself manly in your search for your sister, continue to do so in caring for your mother. Ethel, I'd be glad if you would stay here with Helen, and, Jack,—will you come with me?"

"Of course," replied Mr. Bryant.

"And, King," his father went on, "keep within sound of the telephone. I may call you at any moment. Get your sleep, my boy,—if I should be gone over night,—but sleep here on the library couch, and then the bell will waken you."

"Yes, Father, I'll look after Mother, and I'll be right here if you call me. Where are you going?"

"I don't know, my son. I only know I must hunt for Marjorie with such help and such advice as I can procure. Come on, Jack."

After affectionate farewells, the two men went away.

"First for that conductor," said Mr. Maynard. "I cannot wait till afternoon; I shall try to reach him by telephone or go to his home."

At length he learned that the conductor lived in Asbury Park. He was off duty at that hour, and Mr. Maynard tried to get him by telephone, but the line was out of order.

"To his house we go, then," and the two men boarded the first possible train.

At Asbury Park they found his house, but the conductor's wife, Mrs. Fischer, said her husband was asleep and she never disturbed him at that hour of the day, as he had a long run before him, and needed his rest.

But after a few words of explanation of their quest, the good lady became sympathetic and helpful.

"Of course I'll call him," she cried; "oh, the poor mother! my heart aches for her!"

Mr. Fischer came downstairs, rubbing his eyes. It was about noon, and he was accustomed to sleep soundly until two o'clock.

"Why, yes," he said, in answer to their queries. "I remember that girl. I didn't think much about her,—for a good many children travel alone between stations on the shore road. But, somehow, I don't think that child went to New York,—no, I don't think she did."

"Where did she get off?" asked Mr. Maynard, eagerly.

"Ah, that I don't know. You see, the summer crowds are travelling now and I don't notice individuals much."

"Can't you tell by your tickets?" asked Mr. Bryant.

"No, sir; I don't see's I can. You know, lots of people *did* go to New York on my train, and so, I've lots of New York tickets, but of course I couldn't tell if I had hers. And yet,—seems to me,—just seems to me,—that child got off at a way station."

"Then," said Mr. Maynard, with a businesslike air, "I must telephone or telegraph or go personally to every way station between Seacote and New York. It's a strange case. I can only think my daughter became suddenly demented; I can think of no other reason for her conduct. Can you, Jack?"

"No, Ed, I can't. And yet, Marjorie is a child who always does unexpected things. Some crotchet or whimsey of her childish mind *might* account for this strange freak, quite naturally."

"I can't see how. But we will do what we can. Good-day, Mr. Fischer, and thank you for your help and interest."

CHAPTER X

JESSICA BROWN

Meantime, where was Marjorie?

To go back to where we left her, in the railroad train, she had fallen asleep from utter exhaustion of nerve and body.

But her nap was of short duration. She woke with a start, and found, to her surprise, that she was leaning her head against somebody's shoulder.

She looked up, to see the red-faced man gravely regarding her, though he smiled as their eyes met.

"Feel better, little miss?" he said, and again Marjorie felt a strange repulsion, though he spoke kindly enough.

Her mind was bewildered, she was nervous and frightened, yet she had a positive conviction that she ought not to talk to this strange man. She did not like his face, even if his voice was kind.

"Yes, thank you," she said, in distantly polite tones, and again she squeezed herself over toward the window, and away from her seatmate. She sat up very straight, trying to act as grown-up as possible, and then the train stopped at a large station. There were crowds of people hurrying and scurrying about on the platform, and Marjorie was almost sure she had reached

Carolyn Wells

Jersey City, where she knew she must change for New York.

She wanted to inquire, but the conductor was not in sight, and she didn't like to ask the man beside her.

So she rose, as if to leave the car.

The red-faced man rose also, and stepped back as she passed him. In a moment she found herself on the platform, and the train soon went on. Everything about the station looked unfamiliar, and glancing up, she saw by a large sign that she was at Newark! She had never before been in Newark, though she knew in a general way where it was. She went uncertainly into the station, and looked at the clock. It was after five. Marjorie knew she could take another train, and proceed to Jersey City, and so to New York, but her courage had failed her, and she couldn't bear the thought of travelling any further.

And yet, how could she stay where she was? Also, she began to feel very hungry. The exhaustion caused by her emotional grief, and her wearisome journey, made her feel hollow and faint.

She sank down on a seat in the waiting-room, sadly conscious of her lonely and desolate situation.

She tried to summon anew her natural pluck and independence.

"Marjorie Maynard!" she said, to herself, and then stopped, —overwhelmed by the thought that she had no right even to that name!

Presently a voice beside her said: "Now, little miss, won't you let me help you?"

She turned sharply, and looked the red-faced man in the eyes.

He didn't look very refined, he didn't even look good, but the sound of a friendly voice was like a straw held out to a drowning man.

"How can you help me?" she said, miserably.

"Well, fust off, where've ye set out fur?"

The man was uncultured, but there was a note of sincerity in his speech that impressed Marjorie, now that she was so friendless and alone.

"New York," she replied.

"Why'd ye get out at Newark?"

"I made a mistake," she confessed.

"An' what be ye goin' to do now?"

"I don't know."

"Ah, jest what I thought! An' then ye ask, how kin I help ye?"

"Well, how can you?"

Under the spur of his strong voice, Marjorie's spirits had revived the least bit, and she spoke bravely to him.

"Now, that's more peart-like. Wal, in the fust place I kin take ye home with me, an' my old woman'll keep ye fer the night, an' I guess that's what ye need most."

"Where do you live?"

"'Bout five miles out in the country."

"How do you get there?"

"Wal, I ain't got none o' them autymobiles, nor yet no airship; but I've got a old nag that can do the piece in an hour or so."

"Why do you want to take me home with you?" asked Marjorie, for she couldn't help a feeling that there was something wrong.

"Why, bless your heart, child, bekase you're alone and forlorn and hungry and all done out. An' it's my privit opinion as how ye've run away from home."

"No, not that," said Midget, sadly; "I haven't any home."

"Ye don't say so! Wal, wal, never mind fer to-night. You go 'long with me, an' Zeb Geary, he'll look after ye fer a spell, anyhow."

There was no mistaking the kindness now, and Marjorie looked up into the man's red face with trust and gratitude.

"I'd be glad to go with you and stay till to-morrow," she said; "but first I want to own up that I didn't 'zactly trust you,—but now I do."

"Wal, wal, thet shows a nice sperrit! Now, you come along o' me, an' don't try to talk nor nothin'. Jest come along."

He took Midget's hand, and they went down the steps, and along the street for a block or two, to a sort of livery stable.

"Set here a minute," said Mr. Geary, and he left Marjorie on a bench, which stood outside, against the building.

After a time he returned, with an ancient-looking vehicle, known as a Rockaway, and a patient, long-suffering horse.

"Git in back," he said, and Marjorie climbed in, too tired and sad to care much whither she might be taken.

They jogged along at a fair pace, but Mr. Geary, on the front seat, offered no conversation, merely looking back occasionally, as if to assure himself that his guest was still with him.

After a mile or two, Marjorie began to think more coherently.

She wondered what she would have done if she hadn't chanced to fall in with this kind, if rough, friend.

She wondered whether she could ever have reached Grandma Maynard's house in safety, for the crowds and confusion were much worse than she had anticipated, and in New York they would be worse still.

At any rate, she would gladly accept shelter and hospitality for the night, and continue her journey next day, during the earlier hours.

It was well after six o'clock when the jogging old horse turned into a lane, and finally stopped at a somewhat tumble-down porch. An old woman appeared in the doorway, wiping her hands on her apron.

"Wal, Zeb," she called out, "did ye get back?"

"Yes, Sary, an' I brought ye a visitor for the night."

"A what! Wal, I do declar'!" and Mrs. Geary stepped down and peered into the back seat of the Rockaway. "Who in creation is that?"

"I don't know," returned her husband.

"Ye don't know! I swan, Zeb Geary, you must be plumb crazy! Whar'd ye get her?"

"Thar, thar, now, Sary, don't be askin' questions, but take the pore lamb in, an' cuddle her up some. She's plumb beat out!"

Carolyn Wells

"Come on, dearie," said the old wife, who had caught sight of Marjorie's winsome face and sad eyes. "Come along o' me, —I'll take keer o' ye."

Marjorie let herself be helped from the rickety old vehicle, and went with her hostess, in at the kitchen door.

It wasn't an attractive kitchen, such as Eliza's, at Grandma Sherwood's; it was bare and comfortless-looking, though clean and in good order.

"Now, now, little miss," said Mrs. Geary, hobbling about, "fust of all, let's get some supper down ye. When did ye eat last?"

"This noon," said Marjorie, and then, at the remembrance of the happy, merry luncheon table at Seacote, she put her head down on her arms, and sobbed as if she had never cried before.

"Bless 'ee, bless 'ee, now, my lamb; don't go fer to take on so. There, there, have a sup o' warm milk! Oh, my! my!"

In deference to Mrs. Geary's solicitude, Marjorie tried hard to conquer her sobs, and had finally succeeded, when Mr. Geary came in.

"Don't bother her any to-night, Mother," he said, after a sharp glance at Marjorie; "she's all on edge. Feed her up good, and tuck her into bed."

"Yes, yes; here, my lamb, here's a nice soft-boiled egg for your tea. You'll like that, now?"

"Thank you," said Marjorie, her great, dark eyes looking weird in the dimly lighted kitchen.

After a satisfying supper, Mrs. Geary took the child up to a low, slant-ceiled room, that was as bare and clean as the kitchen. The old woman bathed Marjorie's face and hands with unexpected gentleness, and then helped her to undress. She brought a coarse, plain nightgown of her own, but it was clean and soft, and felt comfortable to the tired child.

Then she was tucked between coarse sheets, on a hard bed, but so weary was she that it seemed comfortable.

Mrs. Geary patted her arm and hummed softly an old hymn-tune, and poor little Marjorie dropped asleep almost at once.

"What do you make of it, Father?" asked the old woman, returning to the kitchen.

"She run away from her home fer some reason. Said she hadn't got no home. Stepmother, I shouldn't wonder. We'll find out to-morrow, an' I'll tote her back."

"Mebbe there'll be a reward."

"Mebbe so. But we'll do our best by her, reward or no. But if so be they is one, I'll be mighty glad, fer I had pore luck sellin' that hay to-day."

"Wal, chirk up, Father; mebbe things'll grow brighter soon."

"Mebbe they will, Sary,—mebbe they will."

In her unaccustomed surroundings, Marjorie woke early. The sun was just reddening the eastern horizon, and the birds were chirping in the trees.

She had that same sinking of the heart, that same feeling of desolation, but she did not cry, for her nerves were rested, and her brain refreshed, by her night's sleep. She lay in her poor, plain bed and considered the situation.

"It doesn't matter," she said, sternly, to herself, "how bad I feel about it, it's true. I'm not a Maynard, and never was. I don't know who I am, or what my name is. And I don't believe I'd better go to Grandma Maynard's. Perhaps she doesn't know I'm not really her granddaughter, and then she wouldn't want me, after all. For I'd have to tell her. So I just believe I'll earn my own living and be self-supporting."

This plan appealed to Marjorie's imagination. It seemed grand and noble and heroic. Moreover, she was very much in earnest, and in this crisp, early morning she felt braver and stronger than she had felt the night before.

"Yes," she thought on, "I ought to earn my living,—for I've no claim on Fa—on Mr. Maynard. Perhaps these people here can find me some work to do. At any rate, I'll ask them."

She jumped up, and dressed herself, for she heard Mr. and Mrs. Geary already in the kitchen.

"My stars!" said her hostess, as she appeared; "how peart you look! Slept good, didn't ye?"

"Fine!" said Midget; "good-morning, both of you. Can't I help you?"

Mrs. Geary was transferring baked apples from a pan to an old cracked platter. Though unaccustomed to such work, Marjorie was quick and deft at anything, and in a moment she had the apples nicely arranged and placed on the table. She assisted in other ways, and chattered gayly as she worked.

Too gayly, Mrs. Geary thought, and she glanced knowingly at her husband, for they both realized Marjorie's flow of good spirits was forced,—not spontaneous.

After breakfast was over, Midget said, "Now, I'll wash up the dishes, Mrs. Geary, and you sit down and take a little rest."

"Land sake, child! I ain't tired. An' you ain't used to this work, I see you ain't."

"That doesn't matter. I can do it, and I must do something to pay for my board,—I have very little money."

"Hear the child talk! Wal, you kin help me with the work, a little, an' then we must come to an understandin'."

Marjorie worked with a nervous haste that betrayed her inexperience as well as her willingness, and after a time the plain little house was in order.

Mr. Geary came in from doing his out-of-door "chores," and Marjorie saw the "understandin'" was about to be arrived at. But she was prepared; she had made up her mind as to her course, and was determined to pursue it.

"Now, fust of all," said Mr. Geary, kindly, but with decision, "what is your name?"

"Jessica Brown," said Marjorie, promptly.

She had already assured herself that as she had no real right to the name she had always used, she was privileged to choose herself a new one. Jessica had long been a favorite with her, and Brown seemed non-committal.

Mr. Geary looked at her sharply, but she said the name glibly, and Jessica was what he called "highfalutin" enough to fit her evident station in life, so he made no comment.

"Where do you live?" he went on.

"I have no home," said Marjorie, steadily; "I am a findling."

"A what?"

"A findling,—from the asylum."

The term didn't sound *quite* right to her,—but she couldn't think of the exact word,—and having used it, concluded to stick to it.

Zeb Geary was not highly educated, but this word, so soberly used, struck his humorous sense, and he put his brawny hand over his mouth to hide his smiles.

"Yep," he said, after a moment, "I understand,—I do. And whar'd ye set out fer?"

"I started for New York, but I've decided not to go there."

"Oh, ye hev, hev ye? An' jes' what do ye calkilate to do?"

"Well, Mr. Geary," Marjorie looked troubled,—"and Mrs. Geary, I'd *like* to stay here for a while. I'll work for you, and you can pay me by giving me food and lodging. I s'pose I wouldn't be worth very much at first, but I'd learn fast,—you know,—I do everything fast,—Mother always said so,—I,—I mean, the lady I used to live with, said so. And I'd try very hard to please you both. If you'd let me stay a while, perhaps you'd learn to like me. You see, I've *got* to earn my own living, and I haven't anywhere to go, and not a friend in the world but you two."

These astonishing words, from the pretty, earnest child, in the dainty and fashionable dress of the best people, completely floored the old country couple.

"Well, I swan!" exclaimed Mr. Geary, while Mrs. Geary said, "My stars!" twice, with great emphasis.

"Please," Marjorie went on, "please give me a trial; for I've been thinking it over, and I don't see what I can possibly do but 'work out.' Isn't that what you call it? And if I learn some with you, I might work out in New York, later on."

"Bless your baby heart!" exclaimed Mrs. Geary, wiping her eyes which were moist from conflicting emotions. "Stay here you shall, if you want to,—though land knows we can't well afford the keep of another."

"Oh, are you too poor to keep me?" cried Marjorie, dismayed. "I don't want to be a burden to you. I thought I could help enough to pay for my 'keep.'"

"So ye kin, dearie,—so ye kin," said old Zeb, heartily. "We'll fix it some way, Mother, at least for the present. Now, Jessiky, don't ye worrit a mite more. We'll take keer on ye, and the work ye'll do'll more'n pay fer all ye'll eat."

This was noble-hearted bluff on Zeb's part, for he was hard put to it to get food for himself and his old wife.

He was what is known as "shif'less." He worked spasmodically, and spent hours dawdling about, accomplishing nothing, on his old neglected farm.

But, somehow, a latent ambition and energy seemed to reawaken in his old heart, and he determined to make renewed efforts to "get ahead" for this pretty child's sake. And meantime, if she liked to think she was helping, by such work as those dainty little hands could do, he was willing to humor her.

Beside all this, Zeb didn't believe her story. He still thought she had run away from a well-to-do home; and he believed it was because of an unloving stepmother.

But he was not minded to worry the child further with questions at the present time, and it was part of his nature calmly to await developments.

"Let it go at that, Mother," he advised. "Take Jessiky as your maid-of-all-work, on trial,"—he smiled at his wife over Marjorie's bowed head,—"an' ef she's a good little worker, we'll keep her fer the present."

"My stars!" said Mrs. Geary, and then sat in helpless

contemplation of these surprising events.

"And I *will* be a good worker!" declared Marjorie, "and perhaps, sometime, we can sort of decorate the house, and make it sort of,—sort of prettier."

"We can't spend nothin'," declared Mr. Geary, "'cause we ain't got nothin' to spend. So don't think we kin, little miss."

"No," said Marjorie, smiling at him, "but I mean, decorate with wild flowers, or even branches of trees, or pine cones or things like that."

A lump came in Midget's throat, as she remembered how often she had "decorated" with these things in honor of some gay festivity at home.

Oh, what were they doing there, now? Had they missed her? Would they look for her? They *never* could find her tucked away here in the country.

And Kitty! What *would* she say when she heard of it? And *all* of them! And Mother,—*Mother!*

But all this heart outcry was silent. Her kind old friends heard no word or murmur of complaint or dissatisfaction. If the forlorn old house were distasteful to Marjorie, she didn't show it; if her room seemed to her uninhabitable, nobody knew it from her. She ran out to the fields, and returned with an armful of ox-eyed daisies, and bunches of clover; and, with some grapevine trails, she made a real transformation of the dingy, bare walls.

"Well, I swan!" Mr. Geary said, when he saw it; and his wife exclaimed, "My stars!"

CHAPTER XI

THE REUNION

After leaving the conductor's house in Asbury Park, Mr. Maynard and Mr. Bryant went to a telephone office, and pursued the plan of calling up every railroad station along the road between Seacote and New York.

But no good news was the result. It was difficult to get speech with the station men, and none of them especially remembered seeing a little girl of Marjorie's description get off the train.

"What can we do next?" asked Mr. Maynard, dejectedly; "I can't go home and sit down to wait for police investigation. I doubt if they could ever find Marjorie. I *must* do something."

"It seems a formidable undertaking," said Mr. Bryant, "to go to each of these way stations; and yet, Ed, I can't think of anything else to do. We have traced her to the train, and on it. She must have left it somewhere, and we must discover where."

Mr. Maynard looked at his watch.

"Jack," he said, "it is nearly time for that very train to stop here. Let us get on that, and we may get some word of her from the trainmen other than the conductor."

"Good idea! and meanwhile we'll have just time to snatch a

Carolyn Wells

sandwich somewhere; which we'd better do, as you've eaten nothing since breakfast."

"Neither have you, old chap; come on."

After a hasty luncheon, the two men boarded at Asbury Park, the same train which Marjorie had taken at Seacote the day before. Conductor Fischer greeted them, and called his trainmen, one by one, to be questioned.

"Sure!" said one of them, at last, "I saw that child, or a girl dressed as you describe, get off this train at Newark. She was a plump little body, and pretty, but mighty woe-begone lookin'. She was in comp'ny with a big, red-faced man, a common, farmer-lookin' old fellow. It struck me queer at the time, them two should be mates."

Mr. Maynard's heart sank. This looked like kidnapping. But the knowledge of where Marjorie had alighted was help of some sort, at least.

After discussing further details of her dress and appearance, Mr. Maynard concluded that it was, indeed, Midget who had left the train at Newark with the strange man, and so he concluded to get off there also.

"We're on the trail, now," said Jack Bryant, cheerily; "we're sure to find her."

Mr. Maynard, though not quite so hopeful, felt a little encouraged, and impatiently the two men sprang off the train at Newark. Into the station they went and interviewed an attendant there.

"Yep," he replied, "I seen that kid. She was with old Zeb Geary, an' it got me, what he was doin' with a swell kid like her!"

"Where did they go?" asked Mr. Maynard, eagerly.

"I dunno. Prob'ly he went home. He lives out in the country, and he takes a little jaunt down to the shore now and then. He's sort of eccentric,—thinks he can sell his farm stuff to the hotel men, better'n any other market."

"How can I get to his house?"

"Wanter see Zeb, do you? Well, he has his own rig, not very nobby, but safe. I guess you could get a rig at that stable 'cross the way. An' they can tell you how to go."

"Couldn't I get a motor-car?"

"Likely you could. Go over there and ask the man."

The station attendant had duties, and was not specially interested in a stranger's queries, so, having rewarded him, as they thought he deserved, the two men hastened over to the livery stable.

"Zeb Geary?" said the stable keeper. "Why, yes, he lives five miles out of town. He leaves his old horse here when he goes anywhere on the train. It's no ornament to my place, but I keep it for the old fellow. He's a character in his way. Yes, he went out last night and a little girl with him."

"Could we get a motor here, to go out there?"

"Right you are! I've good cars and good chauffeurs."

In a few moments, therefore, Mr. Maynard and Mr. Bryant were speeding away toward Zeb Geary, and, as they hoped, toward Marjorie.

While the car was being made ready, Mr. Maynard had telephoned to King that they had news of Marjorie, and hoped soon to find her. He thought best to relieve the minds of the dear ones at home to this extent, even if their quest should prove fruitless, after all.

"I can't understand it," said Mr. Maynard, as they flew along the country roads. "This Geary person doesn't sound like a kidnapper, yet why else would Midget go with him?"

"I'm only afraid it *wasn't* Marjorie," returned Mr. Bryant. "But we shall soon know."

*   *   *   *   *

Marjorie had worked hard all day. Partly because she wanted to prove herself a good worker, and partly because, if she stopped to think, her troubles seemed greater than she could bear.

But a little after five o'clock everything was done, supper prepared, and the child sat down on the kitchen steps to rest. She was tired, sad, and desolate. The slight excitement of novelty was gone, the bravery and courage of the morning hours had disappeared, and a great wave of homesickness enveloped her very soul. She was too lonely and homesick even to cry, and she sat, a pathetic, drooped little figure, on the old tumble-down porch.

She heard the toot of a motor-horn, but it was a familiar sound to her, and she paid no attention to it. Then she heard it again, very near, and looked up to see her father and Cousin Jack frantically waving, as the car fairly flew, over many minor obstacles, straight to that kitchen doorway.

"Marjorie!" cried Mr. Maynard, leaping out before the wheels had fairly stopped turning, and in another instant she was folded in that dear old embrace.

"Oh, Father, Father!" she cried, hysterically clinging to him, "take me home, take me home!"

"Of course I will, darling," said Mr. Maynard's quivering voice, as he held her close and stroked her hair with trembling fingers. "That's what we've come for. Here's Cousin

Jack, too."

And then Midget felt more kisses on her forehead, and a hearty pat on her back, as a voice, not quite steady, but determinedly cheerful, said: "Brace up now, Mehitabel, we want you to go riding with us."

Marjorie looked up, with a sudden smile, and then again buried her face on her father's shoulder and almost strangled him as she flung her arms round his neck. Then she drew his head down, while she whispered faintly in his ear. Three times she had to repeat the words before he could catch them:

"Are you my father?" he heard at last. The fear flashed back upon him that Midget's mind was affected, but he only held her close to him, and said, gently, "Yes, Marjorie darling, my own little girl," and the quiet assurance of his tone seemed to content her.

"Wal, wal! an' who be you, sir?" exclaimed a gruff voice, and Mr. Maynard looked up to see Zeb Geary approaching from the barn.

"You are Mr. Geary, I'm sure," said Cousin Jack, advancing; "we have come for this little girl."

"Wal, I'm right down glad on't! I jest knew that purty child had a home and friends, though she vowed she hadn't."

"And you've been kind to her, and we want to thank you! And this is Mrs. Geary?"

"Yep, that's Sary. Come out here, Mother, and see what's goin' on."

Out of shyness, Mrs. Geary had watched proceedings from the kitchen window, but fortified by her husband's presence, she appeared in the doorway.

Carolyn Wells

"They've been so good to me, Father," said Marjorie, still nestling in his sheltering arms.

"Wal, we jest done what we could," said Mrs. Geary. "I knowed that Jessiky belonged to fine people, but she didn't want to tell us nothin', so we didn't pester her."

"And we ain't askin' nothin' from you, neither," spoke up Zeb. "She's a sweet, purty child, an' as good as they make 'em. An' when she wants to tell you all about it, she will. As fer us, —we've no call to know."

"Now, that's well said!" exclaimed Mr. Bryant, holding out his hand to the old man. "And, for the present, we're going to take you at your word. If you agree, we're going to take this little girl right off with us, because her mother is anxiously awaiting news of her safety. And perhaps, sometime later, we'll explain matters fully to you. Meantime, I hope you'll permit us to leave with you a little expression of our appreciation of your real kindness to our darling, and our gratitude at her recovery."

A few whispered words passed between the two gentlemen, and then, after a moment's manipulation of his fountain pen and checkbook, Mr. Bryant handed to old Zeb Geary a slip of paper that took his breath away.

"I can't rightly thank you, sir," he said, brokenly; "I done no more'n my duty; but if so be's you feel to give me this, I kin only say, Bless ye fer yer goodness to them that has need!"

"That's all right, Mr. Geary," said Cousin Jack, touched by the old man's emotion; "and now, Ed, let's be going."

Mrs. Geary brought Marjorie's hat and her little purse, and in another moment they were flying along the country road toward Newark.

Marjorie said nothing at all, but cuddled into her father's arm, and now and then drew long, deep sighs, as if still troubled.

But he only held her closer, and murmured words of endearment, leaving her undisturbed by questions about her strange conduct.

In Newark they telephoned the joyful news to Mrs. Maynard, and then took the first train to Seacote.

All through the two-hour ride, Marjorie slept peacefully, with her father's arm protectingly round her.

The two men said little, being too thankful that their quest was successfully ended.

"But I think her mind is all right," whispered Mr. Maynard, as Mr. Bryant leaned over from the seat behind. "She has some kind of a crazy notion in her head,—but when she's thoroughly rested and wide awake, we can straighten it all out."

The Maynards' motor was waiting at Seacote station, and after a few moments' ride, Marjorie was again in the presence of her own dear people.

"Mother, *Mother*!" she cried, in a strange, uncertain voice, and flew to the outstretched arms awaiting her.

Though unnerved herself, Mrs. Maynard clasped her daughter close and soothed the poor, quivering child.

"*Are* you my mother?" wailed Marjorie, in agonized tones; "*are* you?"

"Yes, my child, *yes*!" and there was no doubting that mother-voice.

"Then why,—*why* did you tell Mrs. Corey I was a findling?"

"Tell Mrs. Corey *what*?"

"Why, when I was practising, you were talking to her, and I heard you tell her that you took me from an asylum when I was a baby,—and that I didn't really belong to you and Father?"

"Oh, Marjorie! Oh, my baby!" and dropping into the nearest armchair, with Marjorie in her lap, Mrs. Maynard laughed and cried together.

"Oh, Ed," she exclaimed, looking at her husband, "it's those theatricals! Listen, Marjorie, darling. Our Dramatic Club is going to give a play called 'The Stepmother,' and Mrs. Corey and I were learning our parts. That's what you heard!"

"Truly, mother?"

"Truly, of course, you little goosie-girl! And so you ran away?"

"Yes; I couldn't stay here if I wasn't your little girl,—and Father's,—and King's sister,—and all. And you said I was different from your own children and,—"

"There, there, darling, it's all right now. And we'll hear the rest of your story to-morrow. Now, we're going to have some supper, and then tuck you in your own little bed where you belong. Have you had your supper?"

"No,—but I set the table," and Marjorie began to smile at the recollection of the Geary kitchen. "You see, Mother, I've been maid-of-all-work."

"And now you've come back to be maid-of-all-play, as usual," broke in Cousin Jack, who didn't want the conversation to take a serious turn, for all present were under stress of suppressed emotion.

"I say, Mops, you ought to have known better," was King's brotherly comment, but he pulled off her black hair-ribbons in the old, comforting way, and Midget grinned at him.

"Let's dispense with these trappings of woe," said Cousin Jack, dropping the black ribbons in a convenient waste-basket.

So Midget went out to supper without any ribbons, her mop of curls tumbling all over her head and hanging down her shoulders.

"My, but I'm hungry!" she said, as she saw once again her own home table, with its pretty appointments and appetizing food.

"You bet you are!" said King, appreciatively; "tell us what you had to eat in the rural district."

"Boiled beef," said Midget, smiling; "and gingerbread and turnips!"

"Not so awful worse," commented King.

"No? Well, s'pose you try it once! I like these croquettes and Saratoga potatoes a whole heap better!"

"Well, I 'spect I do, too. I say, Mops, I'm glad you didn't break your word to come out and play,—at least, not intentionally."

"No, I never break my word. But I guess if you thought you didn't have any father or mother or brother or sister, you'd forget all about going out to play, too."

"I haven't any brother," said King, looking very sad and forlorn.

"I'll be a brother to you," declared Cousin Jack, promptly; "you behaved like a man, last night, old fellow,—and I'm proud to claim you as a man and a brother."

"Pooh, I didn't do anything," said King, modestly.

"Yes, you did," said his mother. "You were fine, my son. And I never could have lived through to-day without you, either."

"Dear old Kingsy-wingsy!" said Midget, looking at him with shining eyes. And then,—for it was their long-established custom,—she tweaked his Windsor scarf untied.

As this was a mark of deep affection, King only grinned at her and retied it, with an ease and grace born of long practice.

"Well, Mehitabel," said Cousin Jack, "I always said you were a child who could do the most unexpected things. Here you've been and turned this whole house upside down and had us all nearly crazy,—and here you are back again as smiling as a basket of chips. And yet you did nothing for which any one could blame you!"

"Indeed they *can't* blame her!" spoke up Mrs. Maynard; "the child thought I was talking to Mrs. Corey, instead of reading my part in the play. Marjorie sha'n't be blamed a bit!"

"That's just what I said," repeated Cousin Jack, smiling at the mother's quick defense of her child; "why, if anybody told me I was a,—what do you call it?—a findling,—I'd run away, too!"

"Don't run away," said Cousin Ethel, laughing. "I'd have to run with you, or you'd get lost for keeps. And I'd rather stay here. But I think we must be starting for Bryant Bower, and leave this reunited family to get along for awhile without our tender care."

"But don't think we don't realize how much we are indebted to you," said Mr. Maynard, earnestly, for the two good friends in need had been friends indeed to the distracted parents.

"Well, you can have a set of resolutions engrossed and framed for us," said Cousin Jack, "or, better yet, you can give me a dollar bill, in full of all accounts. By the way, Mehitabel, it's lucky you came home from your little jaunt in time for your birthday. I incidentally learned that it will be here soon, and we're going to have a celebration that will take the roof right off this house!"

"All right, Cousin Jack; I'm ready for anything, now that I know I've got a father and mother."

"And a brother," supplemented King, "and *such* a brother!" He rolled his eyes as if in ecstasy at the thought of his own perfections, and Marjorie lovingly pinched his arm.

"And a couple of sisters," added Cousin Ethel; "I like to speak up for the absent."

"Yes, and two dearest, darlingest cousins," said Marjorie, gleefully. "Oh, I think I've got the loveliest bunch of people in the whole world!"

CHAPTER XII

A LETTER OF THANKS

"Mother," said Marjorie, the next day, "what is a bread-and-butter letter?"

"Why, dearie, that's a sort of a humorous term for a polite note of acknowledgment, such as one writes to a hostess after making a visit."

"Yes, that's what I thought. So I'm going to write one to Mrs. Geary."

"You may, if you like, my child; but, you know your father gave those old people money for their care of you."

"Yes, I know; but that's different. And I think they'd appreciate a letter."

"Very well, write one, if you like. Shall I help you?"

"No, thank you. King and I are going to do it together."

"What did you call it, Mops?" asked her brother, as she returned to the library, where he sat, awaiting her.

"A bread-and-butter letter; Mother says it's all right."

"Well, but you had other things to eat besides bread

and butter."

"Yes, but that's just the name of it. Now, how would you begin it, King?"

"'Dear Mrs. Geary,' of course."

"Well, but I want it to be to him, too. He was real nice,—in his queer way. And if he hadn't looked after me, where would I have been?"

"That's so. Well, say, 'Dear Mr. and Mrs. Geary, both.'"

So Marjorie began:

> "Dear Mr. and Mrs. Geary Both:
> This is a bread-and-butter letter—"

"I tell you, Mops, they won't like it. They're not up in social doings, and they won't understand that bread and butter means all the things. I think you ought to put 'em all in."

"Well, I will then. How's this?

> "—and a turnip letter, and a boiled-beef letter, and a baked-apple letter, and a soft-boiled egg letter."

"That's better. It may not sound like the fashionable people write, but it will please them. Now thank them for taking care of you."

> "I thank you a whole heap for being so good to me, and speaking kindly to me in the railroad train, when I wasn't so very polite to you."

"Weren't you, Mops?"

"No; I squeezed away from him, 'cause I thought he was rough and rude."

"Well, you can't tell him that."

"No; I'll say this:

"I wasn't very sociable, Sir, because I have been taught not to talk to strangers, but, of course, those rules, when made, did not know I would be obliged to run away."

"You weren't *obliged* to, Midget."

"Yes I was, King! I just simply *couldn't* stay here if I didn't belong, could I? Could you?"

"No, I s'pose not. I'd go off and go to work."

"Well, isn't that what I did?

"But you were kind and good to me, Mr. Geary and Mrs. Geary Both, and I am very much obliged. I guess I didn't work very well for you, but I am out of practice, and I haven't much talent for houseworking, anyway. *You* seem to have, dear Mrs. Geary."

"That's a sort of a compliment, King. Really, she isn't a very good housekeeper."

"Oh, that's all right. It's like when people say you have musical talent, and you know you play like the dickens."

"Yes, I do. Well, now I'll finish this, then we can go down to the beach."

"And so, dear Mr. and Mrs. Geary Both, I write to say I am much obliged—"

"Oh, my gracious, King, I ought to tell them how it happened. About my mistake, you know, thinking Mother was talking in earnest."

"Oh, don't tell 'em all that, you'll *never* get it done. But I suppose they are curious to know. Well, cut it short."

"You see, dear Mr. and Mrs. Geary Both, I am not a findling, as I supposed."

"That's not findling, Midget,—you mean foundling."

"I don't think so. And, anyway, they mean just the same,—I'm going to leave it.

"I find I have quite a large family, with a nice father and mother, some sisters and a brother. You saw my father. Also, I have lovely cousins and four grand-parents and an uncle. So you see I am well supplied with this world's goods. So now, good-by, dear Mr. and Mrs. Geary Both, and with further thanks and obliges, I am,

Your friend,
MARJORIE MAYNARD."

"P.S. The Jessica Brown was a made-up name."

"Do you think that's all right, King?"

"Yep, it's fine! Seal her up, and write the address and leave it on the hall table, and come on."

And so the "bread-and-butter" letter went to Mr. and Mrs. Geary both, and was kept and treasured by them as one of their choicest possessions.

"I knew she was a little lady by the way she pretended not to notice our poor things," said old Zeb.

"I knew by her petticoats," said his wife.

* * * * *

And so the episode of Marjorie's runaway passed into history. Mrs. Maynard, at first, wanted to give up her part in the play of "The Stepmother," but she was urged by all to retain it, and so she did. As Mr. Maynard said, it was the merest coincidence that Marjorie overheard the words without knowing why they were spoken, and there was no possibility of such a thing ever happening again. So Mrs. Maynard kept her part in the pretty little comedy, but she never repeated those sentences that had so appalled poor Marjorie, without a thrill of sorrow for the child and a thrill of gladness for her quick and safe restoration to them.

And the days hurried on, bringing Marjorie's birthday nearer and nearer.

On the fifteenth of July she would be thirteen years old.

"You see," said Cousin Jack, who was, as usual, Director General of the celebration, "you see, Mehitabel, thirteen is said to be an unlucky number."

"And must I be unlucky all the year?" asked Marjorie, in dismay.

"On the contrary, my child. We will eradicate the unluck from the number,—we will cut the claws of the tiger,—and draw the fangs of the serpent. In other words, we shall so override and overrule that foolish superstition about thirteen being unlucky that we shall prove the contrary."

"Hooray for you, Cousin Jack! I'm lucky to have you around for this particular birthday, I think."

"You're always lucky, Mehitabel, and you always will be. You see, this business they call Luck is largely a matter of our own will-power and determination. Now, I propose to consider thirteen a lucky number, and before your birthday is over, you'll agree with me, I know."

"I 'spect I shall, Cousin Jack. And I'm much obliged to you."

"That's right, Mehitabel. Always be grateful to your elders. They do a lot for you."

"You needn't laugh, Cousin Jack. You're awful good to me."

"Good to myself, you mean. Not having any olive-branches of my own, I have to play with my neighbors'. As I understand it, Mehitabel, you're to have a party on this birthday of yours."

"Yes, sir-ee, sir! Mother says I can invite as many as I like. You know there are lots of girls and boys down here that I know, but I don't know them as well as I do the Craigs and Hester. But at a party, I'll ask them all."

"All right. Now, this is going to be a Good-Luck Party, to counteract that foolish thirteen notion. You don't need to know all about the details. Your mother and I will plan it all, and you can just be the lucky little hostess."

So Marjorie was not admitted to the long confabs between her mother and Cousin Jack. She didn't mind, for she knew perfectly well that delightful plans were being made for the party, and they would all be carried out. But there was much speculation in Sand Court as to what the fun would be.

"I know it will be lovely," said Hester, with a sigh. "You are the luckiest girl I ever saw, Marjorie. You always have all the good times."

"Why, Hester, don't you have good times, too?"

"Not like you do. Your mother and father, and those Bryants just do things for you all the time. I don't think it's fair!"

"Well, your mother does things for you,—all mothers do," said Tom Craig.

"Not as much as Marjorie's. My mother said so. She said she never saw anything like the way Marjorie Maynard is petted. And it makes her stuck up and spoiled!"

"Did your mother say my sister was stuck-up and spoiled?" demanded King, flaring up instantly.

"Well,—she didn't say just that,—but she is, all the same!" And Hester scowled crossly at Midget.

"Why, Hester Corey, I am not!" declared Marjorie. "What do I do that's stuck-up?"

"Oh, you think yourself so smart,—and you always want to boss everything."

"Maybe I am too bossy," said Marjorie, ruefully, for she knew that she loved to choose and direct their games.

"Yes, you are! and I'm not going to stand it!"

"All right, Hester Corey, you can get out of this club, then," said Tom, glaring at her angrily; "Marjorie Maynard is Queen, anyway, and if she hasn't got a right to boss, who has?"

"Well, she's been Queen long enough. Somebody else ought to have a chance."

"Huh!" spoke up Dick; "a nice queen you'd make, wouldn't you? I s'pose that's what you want! You're a bad girl, Hester Corey!"

"I am not, neither!"

"You are, too!"

"Jiminy Crickets!" exclaimed King; "can't this Club get along without scrapping? If not, the Club'd better break up. I'm ashamed of you, Dick, to hear you talk like that!"

"Hester began it," said Dick, sullenly.

"Oh, yes; blame it all on Hester!" cried that angry maiden, herself; "blame everything on Hester, and nothing on Marjorie. Dear, sweet, angel Marjorie!"

"Now, Hester Corey, you stop talking about my sister like that, or I'll get mad," stormed King. "She's Queen of this Club, and she's got a right to boss. And you needn't get mad about it, either."

"You can be Queen, if you want to, Hester," said Midget, slowly. "I guess I am a pig to be Queen all the time."

"No, you're not!" shouted Tom. "If Hester's Queen, I resign myself from this Club! So there, now!"

"Go on, and resign!" said Hester; "nobody cares. I'm going to be Queen, Marjorie said I could. Give me your crown, Marjorie."

Midget didn't want to give up her crown a bit, but she had a strong sense of justice, and it did seem that Hester ought to have her turn at being Queen. So she began to lift the crown from her head, when King interposed:

"Don't you do it, Midget! We can't change Queens in a minute, like that! If we *do* change, it's got to be by election and nomination and things like that."

"It isn't!" screamed Hester; "I won't have it so! I'm going to be Queen!"

She fairly snatched the crown from Marjorie's head, and whisked it onto her own head.

As it had been made to fit Midget's thick mop of curls, it was too big for Hester, and came down over her ears, and well over her eyes.

Carolyn Wells

"Ho! ho!" jeered Dick; "a nice Queen you look! Ho! ho!"

But by this time Hester was in one of her regular tantrums.

"I *will* be Queen!" she shrieked; "I will, I tell you!"

"Come on, Mops, let's go home," said King, quietly.

The Maynard children were unaccustomed to outbursts of temper, and King didn't know exactly what to say to the little termagant.

"All right, we'll go home, too," said Tom; "come on, boys!"

They all started off, leaving Hester in solitary possession of Sand Court.

The child, when in one of her rages, had an ungovernable temper, and, left alone, she vented it by smashing everything she could. She upset the throne, tore down the decorations, and flew around like a wildcat.

Marjorie, who had turned to look at her, said:

"You go on, King; I'm going back to speak to Hester."

"I'm afraid she'll hurt you," objected King.

"No, she won't; I'll be kind to her."

"All right, Midge; a soft answer turneth away rats, but I don't know about wildcats!"

"Well, you go on." And Marjorie turned, and went back to Sand Court.

"Say, Hester," she began a little timidly.

"Go away from here, Stuck-up! Spoiled child! I don't want to see you!"

As a matter of fact, Hester presented a funny sight. She was a plain child, and her shock of red hair was straight and untractable. Her scowling face was flushed with anger, and the gold paper crown was pushed down over one ear in ridiculous fashion.

Marjorie couldn't help laughing, which, naturally, only irritated Hester the more.

"Yes, giggle!" she cried; "old Smarty-Cat! old Proudy!"

"Oh, Hester, don't!" said Midget, bursting into tears. "How can you be so cross to me? I don't mean to be stuck-up and proud, and I don't think I am. You can be Queen if you want to, and we'll have the election thing all right. Please don't be so mean to me!"

"Can I be Queen?" demanded Hester, a little mollified; "can I, really?"

"Why, yes, if the boys agree. They have as much say as I do."

"They don't either! You have all the say! You always do! Now, promise you'll make the boys let me be Queen, or,—or I won't play!"

Hester ended her threat rather lamely, as she couldn't think of any dire punishment which she felt sure she could carry out.

"I promise," said Marjorie, who really felt it was just that Hester should be Queen for a time.

"All right, then," and Hester's stormy face cleared a little. "See that you keep your promise."

"I always keep my promises," said Marjorie, with dignity; "and I'll tell you what I think of *you*, Hester Corey! I think you ought to be Queen,—it *isn't* fair for me to be it all the time. But I think you might have asked me in a nicer way, and not call names, and smash things all about! There, that's what I think!" and Marjorie glared at her in righteous indignation.

"Maybe I ought," said Hester, suddenly becoming humble, as is the way of hot-tempered people after gaining their point. "I've got an awful temper, Marjorie, but I can't help it!"

"You *can* help it, Hester; you don't try."

"Oh, it's all very well for you to talk! You never have anything to bother you! Nothing goes wrong, and everybody spoils you! Why should *you* have a bad temper?"

"Now, Hester, don't be silly! You have just as good a home and just as kind friends as I have."

"No, I haven't! Nobody likes me. And everybody likes you. Why, the Craig boys think you're made of gold!"

Marjorie laughed. "Well, Hester, it's *your* own fault if they don't think you are, too. But how can they, when you fly into these rages and tear everything to pieces?"

"Well, they make me so mad, I have to! Now, I'm going home, and I'm going to stay there till you do as you promised, and get the boys to let me be Queen."

"Well, I'll try—" began Marjorie, but Hester had flung the torn gilt crown on the ground, and stalked away toward home. Midget picked up the crown and tried to straighten it out, but it was battered past repair.

"I'll make a new one," she thought, "and I'll try to make the boys agree to having Hester for Queen. But I don't believe Tom will. I know it's selfish for me to be Queen all the time, and I don't want to be selfish."

Seeing Hester go away, Tom came back, and reached Sand Court just as Midget was about to leave.

"Hello, Queen Sandy!" he called out; "wait a minute. I saw that spitfire going away, so I came back. Now, look here, Mopsy Maynard, don't you let that old crosspatch be Queen!"

"I can't, unless we all elect her," returned Midget, smiling at Tom; "but I wish you would agree to do that. It isn't fair, Tom, for me to be Queen all the time."

"Why isn't it? It's your Club! You got it up, and Hester came and poked herself in where she wasn't wanted."

"Well, we took her in, and now we ought to be kind to her."

"Kind to such an old Meany as she is!"

"Don't call her names, Tom. I don't believe she can help flying into a temper, and then, when she gets mad, she doesn't care what she says."

"I should think she didn't! Well, make her Queen if you want to, but if you do, you can get somebody else to take my place."

"Oh, Tom, don't act like that," and Marjorie looked at him, with pleading eyes.

"Yes, I *will act* like that! Just exactly like that! I won't belong to any Court that Hester Corey is queen of!"

Marjorie sighed. What *could* she do with this intractable boy? And, she almost knew that King would feel the same way. Perhaps, if she could win Tom over to her way of thinking, King might be more easily influenced.

"Tom," she began, "don't you like me?"

"Yes, I do. You're the squarest girl I ever knew."

"Then, don't you think you might do this much for me?"

"What much?"

"Why, just let Hester be Queen for a while."

"No, I don't. That wouldn't be any favor to you."

"Yes, it would. If I ask you, and you refuse, I'll think you're real unkind. And yet you say you like me!"

Marjorie had struck a right chord in the boy's heart. He didn't want Hester for Queen, but still less did he want to refuse Midget her earnest request.

"Oh, pshaw!" he said, digging his toe in the sand; "if you put it that way, I'll *have* to say yes. Don't put it that way, Midget."

"Yes, I *will* put it that way! And if you're my friend, you'll say yes, yourself, and then you'll help me to make the other boys say yes. Will you?"

"Yes, I s'pose so," said Tom, looking a little dubious.

CHAPTER XIII

THIRTEEN!

Marjorie's thirteenth birthday dawned bright and clear.

Her opening eyes rested on some strange thing sticking up at the foot of her bed, but a fully-awakened glance proved it to be a big No. 13, painted on a square of white pasteboard, and decorated with painted four-leaved clovers.

The motto "Good Luck" was traced in ornamental letters, and the whole was in a narrow wood frame.

"That's my birthday greeting from Cousin Jack and Cousin Ethel!" Marjorie said to herself; "I recognize her lovely painting, and it's just like them, anyway. I'll hang that on my bedroom wall, till I'm as old as Methusaleh."

"Happy Birthday, darling!" said her mother, coming in, and sitting on the side of the bed; "many happy returns of the day."

"Oh, dearie Mother! I'm so glad I've got you! and I'm *so* glad you're really my very own mother! Give me thirteen kisses, please, ma'am!"

"Merry Birthday, Midget!" called her father, through the crack of the door. "You two had better stop that love-feast and get down to breakfast!"

Carolyn Wells

So Marjorie sprang up, and made haste with her bathing and dressing, so that in less than half an hour she was dancing downstairs to begin her Lucky Birthday. Her presents were heaped round her plate, and the parcels were so enticing in appearance, that she could scarcely eat for impatience.

"Breakfast first," decreed her father, "or I fear you'll become so excited you'll never eat at all."

So Marjorie contented herself with pinching and punching the bundles, while she ate peaches and cream and cereal.

"Oh, what *is* in this squnchy one?" she cried, feeling of a loosely done-up parcel. "It smells so sweet, and it crackles like silk!"

"Kitty sent that," answered her mother, smiling, "and she wrote me that she made it herself."

But at last the cereal-saucer was empty, and the ribbons could be untied.

Kitty's gift proved to be a lovely bag, of pink and blue Dresden silk.

"What's it for?" asked King, not much impressed with its desirability.

"Oh, for anything!" cried Marjorie. "Handkerchiefs,—or hair-ribbons,—or,—or just to hang up and look pretty."

"Pretty foolish," opined King, but he greeted with joy the opening of the next bundle.

"Jumping Hornets!" he exclaimed; "isn't that a beauty! *Just* what I wanted!"

"Whose birthday is this, anyhow?" laughed Marjorie, as she carefully unrolled the tissue-paper packing from a fine microscope. Uncle Steve had sent it, and it was both valuable and practical, and a thing the children had long wished for.

"Well, you'll let a fellow take a peep once in a while, won't you?"

"Yes, if you'll be goody-boy," said Midget, patronizingly.

Grandma Sherwood's gift was a cover for a sofa-pillow, of rich Oriental fabric, embroidered in gold thread.

"Just the thing for my couch, at home," said Midget, greatly pleased.

"Just the thing to pitch at you, after it gets stuffed," commented King. "Go on, Mops, open the big one."

The big one proved to be a case, from Mother and Father, containing a complete set of brushes and toilet articles for Marjorie's dressing-table. They were plain shapes, of ivory, with her monogram on each in dark blue.

"Gorgeous!" she exclaimed, clapping her hands. "Just what I longed for,—and so much nicer than silver, 'cause that has to be cleaned every minute. Oh, Mothery, they are lovely, and Fathery, too. Consider yourselves kissed thirteen hundred times! Oh, what's this?"

"That's my present," said King. "Open it carefully, Mops."

She did so, and revealed a pincushion, but a pincushion so befrilled and belaced and beflowered one could scarce tell what it was.

"I picked it out myself," said King, with obvious pride in his selection. "I know how you girls love flummadiddles, and I took the very flummadiddlyest the old lady had. Like it, Mops?"

"Like it! I *love* it! I adore it! And it will go fine with this beauty ivory set."

"Yes, you'll have a Louis Umpsteenth boudoir, when you get back to Rockwell."

"I shan't use it down here," said Marjorie, fingering the pretty trifle, "for the sea air spoils such things. But when I get home I'll fix my room all up gay, may I, Mother?"

"I 'spect so. It's time you had a new wallpaper, anyway, and we'll get one with little pink rosebuds to match King's pincushion."

The Bryants' gift came next.

It was in a small jeweller's box, and was a slender gold neck chain and pendant, representing a four-leafed clover in green enamel on gold, on one petal of which were the figures thirteen in tiny diamonds.

"Oh, ho! Diamonds!" cried King. "You're altogether too young to wear diamonds, Mops. Better give it to me for a watch fob."

"I'm not, am I, Father?" said Marjorie, turning troubled eyes to her father.

"No, Midget. Not those little chips of stones. A baby could wear those. And by the way, where is Baby's gift?"

"My p'esent!" cried Rosy Posy, who had sat until now silent, in admiration of the unfolding wonders. "My p'esent, Middy! It's a palumasol!"

"Then it's this long bundle," said Marjorie, and she unwrapped a beautiful little parasol of embroidered white linen.

"Oh, Rosy Posyeums!" she cried. "This is *too booful!* I never saw such a pretty one!"

"Me buyed it! Me and Muvver! Oh, it's *too* booful!" and the baby kicked her fat, bare legs in glee at her own gift.

Grandma and Grandpa Maynard sent a silver frame, containing their photographs, and Grandma sent also a piece of fine lace, which was to be laid away until Marjorie was old enough to put it to use. It was her custom to send such a piece each year, and Marjorie's collection was already a valuable one.

There were many small gifts and cards from friends in Rockwell, and from some of the Seacote children, and when all were opened, Midget begged King to help her take them to the living-room, where they might be displayed on a table.

And then the Bryants arrived, and the house rang with their greetings and congratulations.

"Unlucky Midget!" cried Cousin Jack. "Poor little unlucky Mopsy Midget Mehitabel! Oh, what a sad fate to be thirteen years old, and to be so loaded down with birthday gifts that you don't know where you're at!

> "Mopsy Midget Mehitabel May
> Has come to a most unlucky day!
> Nothing will happen but feasting and fun,
> And gifts,—pretty nearly a hundred and one!
> Jolly good times, and jolly good wishes,
> A jolly good party with jolly good dishes.
> Every one happy and everything bright,
> Good Luck is here—and bad Luck out of sight.
> 'Tis the luckiest day that ever was seen,
> For Marjorie Maynard is just thirteen!"

"Oh, Cousin Jack, what a beautiful birthday poem! I'm sure there *couldn't* be a luckier little girl than I! I've got everything!"

"And we've got *you!*" cried her father, catching her in his arms with a heart full of gratitude that she was safe at home with them.

* * * * *

The party was to begin at four o'clock, and the guests were invited to stay until seven. In good season Marjorie was dressed, and down on the veranda ready to receive her little friends.

She wore a pretty, thin white frock, with delicate embroidery, and the pendant that had been her birthday gift.

The family were all assembled when she came down, and though it would be half an hour before they could expect the guests, they all seemed filled with eager anticipation.

"What's the matter?" asked Midget, looking from one smiling face to another.

"Nothing, nothing!" said King, trying to look unconcerned.

"Nothing, nothing," said Cousin Jack, pulling a wry face.

But Mrs. Maynard said, "There's another birthday surprise for you, Marjorie dear. It has just come, and it's in the living-room. Go and hunt for it."

Marjorie danced into the house, and they all followed. She began looking about for some small object, peering into vases and under books, till her father said:

"Look for something larger, Midget; something quite large."

"And be careful of your frock," warned her mother, for Midget was down on her hands and knees, looking under the big divan.

"Keep on your feet!" advised King. "And look everywhere."

"Pooh! If I keep on my feet, I can't find anything big!" exclaimed Midget. "Where could it be hidden?"

"That's for you to find out!" returned King.

"I'll give you a hint," said Cousin Jack. "Turn, Mehitabel, turn."

Marjorie turned slowly round and round, but that didn't help her any.

"Turn, turn, turn, turn," Cousin Jack kept saying in a monotone, and suddenly it flashed on Marjorie that he meant for her to turn something else beside herself.

She turned the key of a bookshelf door, and opened it, but found nothing but books.

"Turn, turn, turn, turn," droned Cousin Jack.

"Oh," thought Marjorie, "the closet!" and flying to the door of a large closet in the room, she turned the knob, the door flew open, and there she saw,—Uncle Steve and Kitty!

"Oh, Kit!" she cried, and in a moment the two girls were so tangled up that detriment to their party frocks seemed inevitable.

But they were persuaded to separate before too much damage was done, and then Marjorie turned to greet Uncle Steve.

"I daren't rumple your fine feathers," he said, standing 'way off, and extending his fingertips to her. "But I'm *terrible* glad to see you, and to find that you've grown up as good as you are beautiful."

This made Marjorie laugh, for she didn't think she was either.

"How *did* you happen to come?" she cried, for she couldn't

realize that Kitty was really there.

"Oh, it was just a stroke of good luck," said Cousin Jack. "You know to-day is your lucky day."

"'Deed it is!" declared Marjorie. "Come on, Kit, let's go and sit in the swing till the people come to the party."

The sisters had time for a short, merry chat, and then the guests began to arrive. There were about twenty-five boys and girls, and with the grown-ups this made quite a party.

It was fun, indeed, to have both Cousin Jack and Uncle Steve present, for these two men just devoted themselves to the cause, and made so much fun and merriment that they seemed like big children themselves.

They gave a burlesque wrestling match on the lawn that sent the young people off into peals of laughter. They made up funny dialogue, and were always playing good-natured tricks on some of the children. Then Cousin Jack said:

"Now we will play the Good Luck game. Into the hall, all of you!"

The children scampered into the hall, and on the wall they saw a large placard which read:

"Pins	one
Hairpins	two
Four-leafed clovers	five
Horse-shoes	ten
Pennies	fifteen
Black cats	twenty-five."

Each guest was given a small fancy basket, with ribbons tied to the handle. Then they were instructed to hunt all the rooms on the lower floor, the veranda, and the nearby lawns, and gather into their baskets such of the above mentioned articles as they could find. A prize would be given to the one who had the most valuable collection, according to the values given on the placard.

At the word "go!" they scuttled away, and hunted eagerly, now and then stooping to pick up a pin from the floor, or reaching up to get a horseshoe from the mantelpiece. The rooms had been literally sown with the small objects; the clovers and horseshoes being cut from pasteboard and painted, and the black cats being tiny china, wooden, or bronze affairs.

Cousin Jack must have had an immense store of these findings, for the baskets filled rapidly, and yet there seemed always more to be found.

"How are you getting along, Hester?" asked Marjorie as she met her.

"Can't find any hardly. I never have any luck! I s'pose you have a basket full!"

"Nearly," said Marjorie, laughing at Hester's ill-nature in the midst of the others' merriment.

"Say, Hester, I'll tell you what! I'll change baskets with you. Want to?"

"Will you?" and Hester's eyes sparkled. "Oh, Marjorie, will you?"

"Yes, I will, on condition that you'll be nice and pleasant, and not go around looking as cross as a magpie!"

"All right, give me your basket," and Hester put on a very bright smile in anticipation of winning the game.

"What did you do that for?" asked Kitty, who saw the transfer of baskets.

Carolyn Wells

"Oh, because. Never mind now, Kit, I'll tell you to-morrow," and Midget danced away with Hester's almost empty basket hanging from her arm.

She picked up a few more things here and there, and then Cousin Jack rang a bell to announce that the game was over. The baskets, each having its owner's name on a card tied to it, were all put on the hall table, and Mrs. Maynard and Cousin Ethel appraised the contents, while the children went to another game.

This time Uncle Steve conducted affairs. Several tables in the living-room were surrounded by the players, and each was given a paper and pencil.

"I see," Uncle Steve began, "that this is a Good Luck party. So each of you write the words 'good luck' at the top of your paper. Have you done so? Good! Now, I hope you will all of you have all good luck always, but if you can't get it all, get part. So try your hand at it by making words of four letters out of those two words you have written. Use each letter only once,—unless it is repeated, like *o* in 'good.' However, that's the only one that *is* a repeater, so use the others only once in any word you make. The words must be each of four letters,— no more and no less. And they must all be good, common, well-known English words. Now go ahead, and the best list takes a prize."

How the children scribbled! How they nibbled their pencils and thought! How they whispered to each other to ask if such a word was right!

Marjorie was quick at puzzles, but she didn't think it would be polite to take the prize at her own party, so she didn't hand in her list. Neither did Kitty nor King. So when the lists were handed in, Uncle Steve rapidly looked them over.

"The longest list," he announced, "contains ten words."

"Oh, dear!" sighed Hester. "Isn't that just my bad luck! I had nine."

"So did I," said several others, but it was Tom Craig's list that had ten, so he received the prize. His list, as Uncle Steve read it out, was: Cook, loud, duck, cool, cold, lock, look, dock, clod, gold. The prize was a box of candy made in the shape of a four-leafed clover, so it was really four boxes.

Tom generously offered to pass the sweets around at once, but Uncle Steve advised him not to, as supper would be served pretty soon.

The children all liked the game, and clamored for a repetition of it, but Cousin Jack said it was his turn for a game now, and if they'd all stay at the tables, he'd give it to them.

"This is my own game," he said, "because it is called jackstraws, and my name is Jack. I am not a man of straw, however, as you'd soon find if you tried to knock me over! The game is almost like ordinary jackstraws, but with slight additions."

Then there were passed around bunches of jackstraws for each table. They were just like ordinary jackstraws, except they were of different colors, and a little card told how to count. White ones were one; red ones, two; blue ones, five; silver ones, ten; and gold ones, twenty. Then one marked Good Luck counted fifteen, and another, marked *thirteen*, counted twenty-five. This proved that thirteen was *not* an unlucky number!

It's always fun to play jackstraws, and the children went at it with a zest. Midget, at the next table, was not surprised to hear Hester complaining, "Oh, you joggled me! That isn't fair! I ought to have another turn! I *never* have any luck!" Marjorie smiled across at her, and, seeming to remember the condition of the basket exchange, Hester tried to smile, and succeeded fairly well.

Milly Fosdick won that prize, and they all laughed when it

　　　　Carolyn Wells

turned out to be a straw hat of Indian make. It was of gay pattern basket work, and adorned with beads and feathers. Milly was delighted with it, and said she should always keep it as a souvenir.

By that time the ladies had completed their task, and the prize for the Good Luck hunt fell to Hester Corey. This was the prettiest prize of all, being a beautifully illustrated copy of Grimms' "Fairy Tales," and Hester was enchanted with it. She took it eagerly, and never seemed to think for a moment that perhaps it wasn't quite fairly won; nor did she thank Marjorie for the assistance she gave.

Then they all went out to supper. And such a supper as it was! The table was decorated with green four-leafed clovers, and gilt horseshoes, and black cats, and yellow new moons. And every one had a little rabbit's foot, mounted like a charm, for a souvenir; and also a bright lucky penny of that very year.

And the sandwiches were cut like clovers, and the cakes like new moons, and the ice-cream was shaped like horseshoes, and everybody wished everybody else good luck all through Marjorie's thirteenth year. And when the young guests went away they all sang:

"Good luck, ladies; good luck, ladies;
Good luck, ladies;
We're going to leave you now."

CHAPTER XIV

QUEEN HESTER

"Kit's my bestest birthday present," declared Marjorie, as they sat together in the veranda swing the morning after the party.

Kitty pulled her sister's curls in absent-minded affection, and remarked, thoughtfully:

"Mopsy, I don't seem to care much for that red-headed Hester girl."

"She's a queer thing," Marjorie returned, "but I sort of like her, too. You see, Kit, she has a fearful temper, and she can't help being spiteful."

"Oh, fiddlesticks, Mops! Anybody can help being spiteful if they want to."

"No, she can't, Kit. She flies into a rage over nothing. And then she's sorry afterward."

"Will she be at the Sand Court thing, or whatever you call it, to-day?"

"Yes, all the club will be there. Come on, let's go."

The sisters ran down to Sand Court and found King and the Craig boys already there.

Carolyn Wells

"Old Crosspatch hasn't come yet," observed Dick, after they had all said "Hello!"

"Dick," said Midget, "I wish you wouldn't call our Sand Witch such unkind names."

"Well, she *is* a crosspatch."

"Well, never mind if she is. Don't let's call names, anyway."

And then Hester arrived. It was easily seen she was prepared for a fray. She was not smiling, and she said "Hello" with a very sour expression of face. Then she turned to Midget.

"Did you make me a new crown?" she said. "Are you going to let me be Queen?"

"We have to vote about that," returned Marjorie, "and I do hope, my courtiers, that we won't have any squabbling before our royal visitor, Miss Princess Sand,—Sand—well, San Diego is the only name I can think of for Kit!"

"Hail, Princess Sandeago!" cried Tom, and all the courtiers ducked almost to the ground in low bows.

"Now," went on Marjorie, "our first business this morning is the election of a new Queen."

"Queens aren't elected," growled Tom, "they,—they,—what *do* they do? Oh, they succeed!"

"That's exactly what they do!" cried Midget. "And *I'm* going to succeed! I mean I'm going to succeed in my plan of having Hester succeed me! I asked Father about elections, and he said people could be instructed to vote a certain way. So I hereby instruct you all, my beloved courtiers, to vote for a new Queen. The same to be our beloved Sand Witch."

"Beloved grandmother!" exclaimed Tom, irrepressibly.

"No, my Grand Sandjandrum," went on Midget, looking sternly at him, "she isn't your grandmother, but she's to be your new sovereign, so you may as well make up your mind to it."

As Hester began to think Midget was going to make the change, whether the boys wanted to or not, she suddenly became very light-hearted and smiled at everybody.

"I'll be a good Queen," she said, ingratiatingly, "and I'll do whatever you want me to."

And then King waked up to the fact that since Midget desired this change, and since it might have the effect of keeping Hester pleasant and good-natured, perhaps it was a good plan after all. So he said:

"All right; I'll vote as Queen Sandy instructs."

Tom looked at him in surprise, and then, remembering he had practically promised to do as Marjorie asked, he said:

"Well, I will too. But only on condition that the new Queen promises to be pleasant and nice all the time."

"I will," declared Hester, earnestly, her face fairly radiant now at the thought of wearing the crown.

"You ought to take an oath of office and say so," advised Kitty, who was critically watching the proceedings.

"What's that mean?" demanded Hester.

"Why, swear that you won't lose your temper."

"Oh, I wouldn't *swear*!" cried Hester, in dismay.

"Kit doesn't mean bad swearing," explained King. "She means official swearing, or something like that. All Queens do it, and juries, and presidents, and everything. It's only promising or vowing."

"Well, I'll promise or vow," agreed Hester, "but I won't swear."

"All right," said Marjorie. "You must hold up both hands, and say 'I promise or vow to be a good Queen and not get mad at my courtiers.' Say it now."

So Hester raised both hands as high as she could and repeated Marjorie's words.

"Now you've taken your oath of office, and you're queen," said Kitty, who was unconsciously taking charge of affairs. "Where's the crown, Mops?"

"The new Queen tore it up the other day," said Midget, demurely.

"Then she must make a new one," commanded Kitty. "Never mind; for to-day this will do."

The Princess San Diego hastily twisted some vines into a wreath, and laid it gently on the brilliant locks of the new Queen.

"I crown you Queen Sandy!" she said, dramatically.

"It's all right, Kit," said King, looking quizzical, "but just how do you happen to be running this court?"

"Oh, I might as well," returned Kitty carelessly. "I don't think the rest of you are very good at it."

"That's so," admitted Tom. "I guess we do squabble a lot."

"It isn't only that," said Kitty, "but you don't have much order and ceremony."

"I've noticed that," put in Dick. "We just talk every-day sort of talk. I think we ought to be grander."

"So do I," agreed Kitty. "Here, Hester, give me that crown; I'll be Queen for to-day, and show you how."

There was nothing bumptious or even dictatorial in Kitty's manner; she merely wanted to show them how a Queen ought to act. So she put the vine wreath on her own head, and breaking a branch from a tall shrub nearby for a sceptre, she seated herself on the dilapidated throne.

"I pray you sit," she said, condescendingly, to her court. "Ha! where is my page?"

"There is no page, O Queen," said the Grand Sandjandrum, looking mortified.

"Thus I create one!" announced Kitty, calmly. "Sand Crab, kneel before me!"

Harry sprang forward to obey, and kneeled at Kitty's feet.

"Thus I anoint thee page!" declared the Queen, dramatically tapping him three times on his shoulder. "Rise, Sir Page, and attend upon me!"

"Yes, ma'am! What shall I do?" asked the new page, greatly flustered.

"Stand thou here at my right hand. It may be I might have an errand or two now and then."

"Aye, aye, O Queen!" declaimed Dick, who was catching the spirit of Kitty's rule.

"Well spoke, fair sir. Stand thou there, I prithee. And now, Courtiers, is there any business to be discussed?"

Carolyn Wells

"Nay, O Queen," said Tom, "we but wait thy pleasure."

"Then my pleasure is now to install the new Queen. And, prithee, my courtiers, when that the new Queen is enthroned, then does the receding Queen become the Sand Witch?"

"Yea, O fair Queen," said Marjorie, coming up with mincing steps and bowing before Kitty. "From now on I am the Sand Witch of this court, and I humbly beg thy favor."

"Favor be thine!" announced the temporary Queen. "And now, O my courtiers, lead to me Queen Hester Sandy, Queen of Sand Court!"

Reconciled at last to this state of things, King and Tom sprang to escort Hester. Dick and Harry marched gravely behind, while Midget stalked along ahead, and thus quite an imposing procession approached Queen Kitty and ranged themselves before her.

"O Queen," Kitty began, "you have already taken oath of office, O Queen! So now naught remains but to take the seat of royalty, the honored throne of Sand Court, O Queen!"

And then Hester scored her success. She stepped up on the sand mound that was the throne, and bowed her head while Kitty transferred the vine wreath that represented the crown. Then Hester drew herself up majestically, waved her sceptre, and declaimed:

"I, the Queen of Sand Court, accept this honor that is thus thrust upon me!"

There were some astonished faces among the courtiers at this speech, but nobody interrupted.

"I, Queen Sandy, promise to be a good Queen to my beloved courtiers, and never to lose my temper or speak cross, but to emulate the sweet and sunlighty disposition of our departing and beloved Queen, who is now a Sand Witch. Wherefore, my courtiers, I beseech your fealty and faith, and I present my compliments, and the compliments of this court to our visitor, the Princess San Diego. This lovely lady has been a great help, and we now salute her. I bid thee all salute!"

They all saluted by bowing low to Kitty; indeed, the page bowed so low that he tumbled over, but soon scrambled up again.

"And now," went on Queen Sandy, "I bid thee salute our Sand Witch. She is a witch of goodness and joy. We all love her, the court honors her, and one and all we now salute her!"

More low bows followed, and then the court resumed its upright attitude and awaited orders.

"There is no more saluting necessary," explained the gracious Queen. "You boy courtiers can't expect it. Now the court is dismissed and the Sand Club will play something."

The Queen came down from the throne, and courtly manners and speeches were laid aside.

"Let's fix up the court instead of playing," suggested Kitty, and as all thought this a good idea, they went at it.

Everybody worked with a will, for it was fun to get the court in order again, and Kitty and Midget were so fond of fixing up and decorating that when the task was over, Sand Court was far handsomer than ever before.

Shell borders outlined the throne and the courtier's seat, and the old legless chair was so draped with cheesecloth and green vines that it was a picture in itself. Then it was luncheon time, and the courtiers said good-bye and parted to go to their homes.

"She's a funny girl," said Kitty, as the Maynard trio reached their house. "As soon as she got what she wanted, she was sweet as pie. But if you hadn't given up the Queen to her, Mops, she would have been madder'n hops."

"I know it," said Midget, "but that wasn't the reason I did it. I did it 'cause I thought it was fairer for her to have a turn at being Queen."

"And it was," said Kitty, judicially. "I think you did right, Mopsy; but, all the same, she'll never keep that promise to be sweet and pleasant."

"Oh, Kitty, she'll have to! Why, she vowed it!"

"Oh, pshaw, she'll get mad and forget all about that vow. Say, Mops, what do you think? I've learned to make cake."

"You have! Who taught you?"

"Eliza did, up at Grandma's. It was fine. I'll teach you, if you like."

"Do!" urged King. "Then Midge can make little cakes for the Sand Club. Ellen makes 'em sometimes, but she says it's a bother."

Permission being granted by Mrs. Maynard, the girls tried cake-making that very afternoon.

"I'll help yez, shall I?" asked Ellen, as the two energetic damsels raided her pantry.

"No, Ellen," said Marjorie. "Miss Kitty is going to teach me. You go,—go—why, Ellen, you take an afternoon out!"

"It isn't me day out, Miss Midget, but I'll go to me room, an' if yez wants me, yez can send Sarah afther me, sure."

"Can I help?" asked King, who wanted to be in the fun.

"Yes, you can stone raisins," said Kitty, kindly.

At home in Rockwell, Marjorie had always been chief directress in all their doings, but down here Kitty was more like a visitor, and the others politely deferred to her. So King went contentedly to work, stoning raisins, and the girls made the cake.

"I didn't bring my recipe book," said Kitty, "but I guess I remember how to make it. You see, Eliza is going to teach me to make lots of things, so I've quite a big book for recipes."

"How many have you so far?" asked Midget, greatly interested.

"Well, only this one; but it's sponge cake, you know. I shall have more later."

"Yes, of course," said Midget, politely, and suddenly feeling that her younger sister was getting very grown-up, with her recipe book and her sponge cake.

"Now," proceeded Kitty, "if I'm to show you, Midget, you must pay close attention."

"I will,—oh, I will!"

"First, you break the eggs, and separate them, white from yolk, like this,—see!"

But whether she was rattled at having such an interested audience, or whether she was not very expert as yet, Kitty couldn't make the eggs "separate" neatly. Every one she broke persisted in spilling out its yellow and white together.

"Let me try," said Marjorie, but her efforts were not much more successful. Bits of shell would fall in the bowl, and even if she got most of the white in safely, some yellow would spill in, too.

Carolyn Wells

"Does it matter much?" asked King.

"Oh, I don't believe so," said Kitty. "I guess we'll beat the eggs all up together, white and yellow both."

Kitty put in the Dover eggbeater with an air of experience, and whisked its wheel "round and round."

"Let me in, too," said Midget. "There's another beater I found in the cupboard."

There was room in the big bowl for both beaters, and the two girls whizzed the wheels around like mad.

"Hold on!" cried King. "You're flirting that yellow stuff all over!"

"Well, anyway, it's well beaten," declared Kitty, looking at the frothy yellow mass with satisfaction. "Now we put in the flour,—no, the sugar, I think."

"Butter?" suggested Marjorie.

"No, there's no butter in it. This is *sponge* cake."

Properly subdued, Marjorie awaited orders.

"Sugar," Kitty decided at last; "and bring a cup."

Midget brought the cup, and Kitty measured the sugar, and dumped it into the bowl of egg.

"I can't think whether it's three or four cups full," she said, holding a cup full uncertainly over the bowl.

"Dump it in!" advised King. "I like 'em pretty sweet."

So in went the sugar, and Midget was allowed to stir, while Kitty measured flour.

"We have to sift this four times," she announced, with an air of great wisdom. "I'll do this part."

She did, but she was so energetic about it, and the flour sieve so uncertain on its three iron legs, that much of the flour flew over the table, the floor, and the clothing of the workers.

"Hold up, Kit!" cried Marjorie, as a cloud of flour almost blinded her. "I can't see to beat, if you fly that flour around so!"

"Well, it has to be sifted four times," apologized Kitty, and turned it into the sieve again.

Much was lost in transit, and King declared it was already sifted as fine as it would ever be, but Kitty was unmoved by comment or criticism.

"Now it's all right," she said, peering into the pan of finally prepared flour, and ignoring the white dust that was all over everything. "But first a cup of hot water must go in."

"I'll pour it," said King, rising quickly, and taking the tea-kettle from Kitty, who was in imminent danger of scalding herself.

"Just a cup full!" said Kitty, warningly, as the hot water ran over the brimming cup and fell to the floor.

"Never mind," said King, "we'll only use what's in the cup," and carrying it as carefully as possible he poured it into the bowl of batter that Marjorie was faithfully beating.

"Oh, not all at once!" cried Kitty. "It should have been put in little by little."

"Can't help it now," said Midget, cheerfully. "I guess it won't matter. Now in with the flour, Kit; and you must have baking powder."

"I don't think Eliza put in any baking powder," said Kitty, dubiously.

"Oh, she *must* have!" said Midget. "That's what baking powder is for,—to bake with. It's on that shelf, Kitty."

Kitty was uncertain about the baking powder, so took Marjorie's advice.

"But I don't know how much," she said, as she opened the tin box.

"About a tablespoonful to a cup of flour," said Marjorie. "I think I heard Mother say that once." She was not at all sure, but she greatly wanted to help Kitty if possible.

"All right," said Kitty, and having already put in three cups of flour, she added to the mixture three heaping tablespoonfuls of baking powder.

"Now for the raisins," she said.

"I didn't know sponge cake ever had raisins in it," said Marjorie.

"It doesn't, usually," said Kitty, "but I thought it would add an extra touch."

She stirred them in, and then they poured the batter into a cake tin.

"It does look lovely," said Midget, tasting it with a spoon. "It tastes pretty good, but not as good as it looks. I guess it'll be lovely when it's baked. Open the oven, King."

King threw open the oven door with a flourish, and the girls pushed the big pan inside.

"Shut it quick!" warned Kitty. "The cake falls unless you do! It must bake three-quarters of an hour."

And then they all waited patiently for the time to take it out.

Carolyn Wells

CHAPTER XV

A MOTOR RIDE

"Isn't it done yet?" asked King, after half an hour had elapsed.

"Nope," returned Kitty, positively. "It can't be done till three-quarters of an hour, and it's only a half."

"Smells done!" exclaimed Marjorie, sniffing "I believe it's burning, Kit."

"Pshaw, it can't be burning. That isn't a hot fire, is it, King?"

"No," replied King, after removing one of the range covers and scrutinizing the fire. "That's what the cook books call a moderate fire."

"Then that's all right," and Kitty wagged her head in satisfaction. "Sponge cake requires a mod-rit fire."

"But it's leaking out, Kitty!" cried Marjorie, dancing about the kitchen. "Oh, look, it's leaking out!"

Sure enough, smoke was coming out through the edges of the oven door, and a sticky substance began to ooze through.

"The door isn't shut quite tight," began Kitty, but before she could finish, King flung the oven door wide open.

"Better see what's up!" he said, and as the smoke poured out in a volume, and then cleared away a little, a strange sight confronted them.

The cake dough had apparently multiplied itself by ten, if not more. It had risen and run all over the sides of the pan, had dripped down through the grating to the bottom of the oven, and had bubbled up from there all over the sides and door. In fact the oven was lined with a sticky, sizzling, yellow material that had turned brown in some places, and was burned black in others.

"Something must have gone wrong," said Kitty, calmly, as she looked at the ruins. "I was almost sure it didn't need any baking powder. That's what blew it up so."

"H'm," said King. "I don't believe I care for any. Wonder what became of the raisins?"

"You can see them here and there," said Marjorie. "Those burned black spots are raisins. Phew! how it smokes! I'm going out."

"Let's call Ellen," said Kitty, "she said to."

Being summoned, Ellen arrived on the scene of action.

"Arrah, Miss Kitty," she said; "shure, an' I thought ye cuddent make cake. Now, why did ye thry, an' put all in such a pother? Belikes ye want to make me throuble."

"No, Ellen," said Kitty, smiling at her. "I didn't do it purposely for that. I thought it would be good. You see, I did make it once, and it was good."

"Ah, go 'long wid yez,—all of yez! Shure I'll be afther clanin' up. An' niver a shcold I'll shcold yez if ye'll kape outen o' my kitchen afther this."

"Good for you, Ellen!" shouted King. "I thought you'd raise a row! Nice Ellen, good Ellen! Good-bye, Ellen!"

"Good-bye, ye bad babies! I'll make ye some tea-cakes now as ye can eat!"

"Isn't she a duck!" exclaimed Kitty.

"Oh, that's 'cause you're sort of company. If you hadn't been here, and we'd done that she'd have tuned up, all right!"

This was King's opinion, and Marjorie agreed with him. "We never go in the kitchen," she said. "I guess Ellen was so surprised she didn't know *what* to say."

"Well," said Kitty, quite undisturbed by the circumstances, "you see, at Grandma's, Eliza helps me, and sort of superintends what I put in."

"Yes, I see," said King. "Now you do a lot of cooking after you get back there, Kit, and try to learn your recipes better."

Kitty laughed and promised, and then the three children wandered into the dining-room to see what their elders were doing.

"Can't we start at once?" Cousin Ethel was saying. "Oh, here are the kiddies now! Come in, you three blessings in disguise! Do you want to go on a jamboree?"

"What's that?" asked Kitty.

"Oh, a lovely motor ride, with two cars, and stay all night, and lots of lovely things like that!"

"Oh, goody!" cried Marjorie. "Are we really going? Mother's been talking about a trip like that!"

"I guess we will," said Mr. Maynard. "We haven't had an

Ourday for some time. How would you like to take the opportunity for one while we have Kitty-girl among us?"

"Gorgiferous! Gay!" cried Marjorie, and King threw his cap high in the air and caught it deftly on his head.

"When do we start?"

"As soon as we can get off," said Mr. Maynard, looking at his watch. "Scamper, you kiddies, and get into appropriate rigs."

"Oh, what fun!" cried Marjorie, as they flew upstairs. "What shall we wear, Mothery?"

"You'll find your frocks laid out in your rooms," said Mrs. Maynard, who was prepared for this question. "Then put on your motor coats and take your motor bonnets with you,—but you needn't wear them unless you choose."

The girls danced away, and soon were in full regalia. They went flying downstairs to learn more of the particulars of the trip. Nurse Nannie and Rosy Posy were on the porch waiting, the little one greatly excited at thought of the journey.

"Oh, what a grand Ourday, Father!" cried Midget, giving him one of her most ferocious "bear hugs." "We have so much vacation down here, I thought we wouldn't catch any Ourdays!"

"Well, this is an extra thrown in for good measure. I suppose you don't care, Midget, which car you ride in?"

"Not a bit! We keep together, don't we?"

"Yes, as much as possible. Cousin Jack will drive his own car, and Pompton, of course, will drive ours."

"It all happened so swift I can hardly realize it," said Kitty. "Only a minute or two ago I was making cake in the kitchen, and now here I am!"

"Making *what?*" asked King, teasingly, but when he saw Kitty look red and embarrassed he turned the subject.

Kitty had told her mother about the cake episode, but Mrs. Maynard said it was an accident due to inexperience, and nothing further need be said about it.

"I'll divide up the passengers," said Cousin Jack as, with the two cars standing in front of the door, no one knew just which to get in.

"Ethel and I will take Marjorie and King with us, for I think Kitty will want to ride with her mother, and Babykins, too."

"All right," agreed Mr. Maynard, and then he packed Uncle Steve and Mrs. Maynard and Kitty on the back seat, Nannie and Rosamond next in front, and he climbed up beside Pompton.

Some suitcases and a basket of light luncheon were stowed away, and off they started, Ellen and Sarah waving to them from the steps as they flew down the drive. It was a perfect day for motoring. Not too hot, not too breezy, and no dust.

Their destination was Lakewood, but for quite a distance their road lay along by the shore before they turned inland.

Marjorie sat back, beside Cousin Ethel, and King sat in front with Cousin Jack.

"Let's play Roadside Euchre," said Midget.

"We go too fast for that," said King. "We couldn't see the things to count them."

"What is it, Mehitabel?" asked Cousin Jack. "We aren't going so very fast."

"Why, you count the things on each side of the road. You and I are on the right, you know, Cousin Jack, so we count all on this side. Then Cousin Ethel and King count all on their side."

"All what?"

"Well, a horse and vehicle counts one; a vehicle with two horses counts two; and a horse without any wagon or carriage counts five. An automobile counts ten; a herd of cows, fifteen; and a load of hay, twenty. A cat in a window counts twenty-five, and people count five apiece. Any animal, not a horse counts ten."

"But, as I am driving," said Cousin Jack, "I can turn either side, and so make them count as I like."

"No, you must turn just as you would, anyway. Of course, as you turn to the right, King and Cousin Ethel will count most of the vehicles we pass; but we'll make up some other way. Oh, here's a flock of chickens! I forgot to tell you, chickens count one each."

The motor seemed to go right through the flock of chickens, but Cousin Jack was a careful driver and didn't harm one of them. There was a terrific squawking and peeping and clucking as the absurd bipeds ran about in an utterly bewildered manner. The children and Cousin Ethel managed to count them fairly well, but Cousin Jack had to manage his motor.

"How many?" he asked as the last hen was left behind.

"Fourteen for our side," announced Midget, triumphantly.

"And nine for us," said King. "Never mind, we'll make up later."

But they kept fairly even. To be sure, when they met motor-cars, or any vehicles, they had to turn out to the right, which

Carolyn Wells

gave the count to King's side.

But on the other hand, motors sometimes passed them from behind, and if they went along on the right side they were Marjorie's count. Houses were as apt to be on one side as the other, and these added their count of dogs, cats, chickens, and cows, as well as occasional human beings.

Going through small towns was the most fun, for then it required quick counting to get all that belonged to them.

A flock of birds on either side was counted, but a flock of birds that crossed their path was omitted, as it would have counted the same for each.

The game grew more and more exciting. Sometimes one side would be more than a hundred ahead, and then the balance would swing back the other way. About six o'clock they neared Lakewood.

"The game stops as we turn into the main street," said Cousin Jack, "and the prize is this: whichever of you two children win shall select the dessert at the hotel dinner to-night."

"All right," said Marjorie, "but it isn't only us children. We each have a partner who must help us in the selection."

Cousin Jack agreed to this, and in a moment the car swung into the main street of Lakewood.

Midget and King, who had kept account of their hundreds on a bit of paper, began to add up, and it was soon found that Marjorie and Cousin Jack's side had won by about two hundred points.

"Good work!" cried King. "We losers congratulate you, and beg you'll remember that we love ice cream!"

They were following the Maynards' *big* car, and soon both cars stopped and all alighted and went into a beautiful hotel called "Holly-in-the-Woods."

"Oh, how lovely!" whispered Marjorie to Kitty, as she squeezed her sister's arm. "Isn't this fun, Kit?"

"I should say so!" returned Kitty. "The best Ourday ever!"

Then the children were whisked away to tidy up for dinner, and fresh white frocks were found in the suitcases. Midget and Kitty tied each other's ribbons, and soon were ready to go downstairs again. The Bryants met them in the hall, and took them down.

"Isn't it like Fairyland!" said Marjorie, enchanted by the palms and flowers and lights and music. She had never before been in such an elaborate hotel, and she wanted to see it all.

They walked about, and looked at the various beautiful rooms, and then Mr. and Mrs. Maynard came, and they all went to the dining-room.

A table had been reserved for them, and Marjorie felt very grown up and important as the waiter pushed up her chair. After their long ride, their appetites were quite in order to do justice to the good things put before them, and when it was time for dessert, Cousin Jack announced that he and Marjorie were a committee of two to select it.

"Though of course," he added, "any one who doesn't care for what we choose is entirely at liberty to choose something else."

So the two gravely studied the menu, and kept the others in suspense while they read over the long list. Many names were in French, but Marjorie skipped those.

"Ice cream," Kitty kept whispering, in low but distinct stage whispers; and at last Cousin Jack proposed to Midget that they choose what was billed as a "Lakewood Souvenir."

Marjorie had no idea what this might be, but she agreed, for she felt sure it was something nice.

And so it was, for it turned out to be ice cream, but so daintily put up in a little box that it was like a present. The box was carved with crinkly paper, and had a pretty picture of Lakewood scenery framed in gilt on the top. After every one had eaten his ice cream, the boxes were carried away as souvenirs.

Then they all went out and sat on the terrace while the elders had coffee. The three children did not drink coffee, so they were allowed to run around the grounds a little.

"How long are we going to stay here?" asked Kitty.

"Till to-morrow afternoon, I think," replied King. "I heard Father say he thought he'd do that."

"I think it's beautiful," said Midget, "but I'd just as lieve be riding, wouldn't you, Kit?"

"Oh, I don't care. I like 'em both,—first one and then the other."

Kitty was of a contented disposition, and usually liked everything. But the other two were also easily pleased, and the three agreed that they didn't care whether they were motoring or staying at the lovely hotel.

"Now, then, little Maynards, bed for yours!" announced their father, as he came strolling out to find them.

"Father," said Marjorie, grasping his hand, "is this really an Ourday?"

"Yes, Midget; of course it is. You don't mind the Bryants sharing it, do you?"

"No, not a bit. Only,—to-morrow can't I ride with you? If it's our Ourday, I like better to be by you."

"Of course you can!" cried Mr. Maynard, heartily. "We'll fix it somehow."

"But don't tell Cousin Ethel and Cousin Jack that I don't want to ride with them," went on Midget, "because it might hurt their feelings. But you know,—when I thought I didn't have any father,—I thought about all our Ourdays, and—"

Midget's voice broke, and Mr. Maynard caught her to him.

"My darling little girl," he said, "I'm so glad you're back with us for our Ourdays, and you shall ride just where you want to."

"Let her take my place," said Kitty, kindly. "I'd just as lieve go in the other car, and I don't wonder Midget feels like that."

So it was settled that Kitty should ride with the Bryants next day, and then the three children were sent to bed, while the elders stayed up a few hours later.

The girls had a large room, with two beds, and with a delightful balcony, on which a long French window opened.

"Isn't it wonderful?" said Marjorie, softly, as she stepped over the sill, and stood in the soft moonlight, looking down on the hotel flower gardens.

"Yes, indeedy," agreed Kitty; "I say, Mops, I'd like to jump down, flip! into that geranium bed!"

"Oh, Kitty, what a goose you are! Don't do such a thing!"

"I'm not going to. I only said I'd like to; and I'd play it was a sea,—a geranium sea, and I'd swim around in it."

Carolyn Wells

"Kit, you're crazy! Come on to bed, before you do anything foolish."

"I'm not going to do it, really, Mops! but I like to imagine it. I'd waft myself off of this balcony, and waft down to the scarlet of the geraniums and fall in."

"Yes, and be picked up with two broken legs and a sprained ankle!"

"Well—and then I'd see a little boat, on the red geranium sea,—I'd be a fairy, you know,—and I'd get in the little boat—"

"You come and get in your little bed, Miss Kitty," said Nannie, from the window, and laughing gayly, the two girls went in and went to bed.

"Anyway, I'm going to dream of that red geranium bed," announced Kitty, as she cuddled into the smooth, white sheets.

"All right," said Midget, drowsily; "dream anything you like."

CHAPTER XVI

RED GERANIUMS

Wearied by the journey, and the fun of it, Marjorie fell at once into a deep, quiet sleep. Kitty's sleep was deep, too, but not quiet. The child tossed around and waved her arms, muttering about a geranium sea, and a little boat on it.

Nurse Nannie puttered about the room for some time, picking up things, and laying out the girls' clothes for the next day. Then she put out the lights and went away to her own room.

It was, perhaps, ten o'clock when Kitty threw back the bedclothing, and slowly got out of bed. She was sound asleep, and she walked across the room with a wavering, uncertain motion, but went straight to the French window, which was still part way open.

Kitty had sometimes walked in her sleep before, but it was not really a habit with her, and the family had never thought it necessary to safeguard her.

It was a still, warm night, and when she stepped out on the balcony, there was no breeze or waft of cool air to awaken her.

She paused at the low rail of the little balcony, and murmured, "Oh, the lovely soft red flowers! I will lie down on them!" and over the railing she went, plump down into the geranium bed!

Carolyn Wells

As is well known, a fall is not apt to hurt a somnambulist, for the reason that in sleep the muscles are entirely relaxed; but the jar woke Kitty, and she found herself, clad only in her little white nightgown, lying in the midst of the red blossoms.

She did not scream; on the contrary, she felt a strange sense of delight in the odorous flowers and the scent of the warm, soft earth.

But in a moment she realized what had happened, and scrambled up into a sitting posture.

"My gracious! it's Kit!" exclaimed a voice, and from among the group of people on the veranda Cousin Jack ran down to her. The others followed, and in a moment Kitty was surrounded by her own people. She flew to her mother's arms, and Cousin Ethel quickly drew off her own evening wrap and put it around Kitty.

"How *did* you happen to fall?" asked her father, who soon saw she was not hurt, or even badly jarred.

"I was asleep, I guess," Kitty returned; "anyway I dreamed that I wanted to jump in the red geranium sea,—so I jumped."

"You jumped! out of the window?"

"Yes,—that is, off of the little balcony. You see, I was asleep until I landed. Then I found out where I was."

Kitty was quite calm about it, and cuddled into the folds of Cousin Ethel's satin cloak, while she told her story.

"Of course, I shouldn't have jumped if I had been awake," she said; "but you can't help what you do in your sleep, can you?"

"No," said Uncle Steve; "you weren't a bit to blame, Kitsie, and I'm thankful you came down so safely. But I think that window must be fastened before you go to sleep again. One such escapade is enough for one night."

The other guests on the veranda looked curiously at the group, but Kitty was protected from view by her own people, and, too, the big cloak hid all deficiencies of costume.

"Well, we have to get used to these unexpected performances," said Mr. Maynard, "but I do believe my children are more ingenious than others in trumping up new games."

"We are," said Kitty, "but usually it's Midget who does the crazy things. King and I don't cut up jinks much."

"That's so," agreed Uncle Steve. "Last summer Miss Mischief kept us all in hot water. But this year, Kitsie has been a model of propriety. She never walks out of second-story windows when she's at our house. I guess I'd better take her back there."

"Not to-morrow," said Kitty. "Wait till next day, won't you, Uncle Steve?"

"All right; day after to-morrow, then. But we mustn't stay away from Grandma longer than that."

"And now I think our adventurous little explorer must go back to her dreams," said Mrs. Maynard. "Who wants to carry her upstairs?"

As Uncle Steve was the biggest and strongest of the three men, he picked up the young sleepwalker, and started off with her. Mrs. Maynard followed, and they soon had Kitty safely in bed again, with the French window securely fastened against any further expeditions.

The mother sat by the little girl until she went to sleep, and this time her slumber was untroubled by dreams of geranium seas with fairy boats on them.

Next morning, Marjorie was greatly interested in Kitty's story.

"Oh, Kit," she exclaimed, "I wish I had seen you step off! Though, of course, if I *had* seen you, you wouldn't have done it! For I should have waked you up. Well, it's a wonder you didn't smash yourself. Come on, let's hurry down and look at that flower bed."

But by the time the girls got down there, the hotel gardener had remade the flower bed, and it now looked as if no one had ever set foot on it.

"Pshaw!" said Marjorie, "they've fixed it all up, and we can't even see where you landed. Did it make a big hole, Kit?"

"I don't know, Mops. About as big as I am, I suppose. Can't you imagine it?"

Marjorie laughed. "Yes, I can imagine you landing there, in your nightgown and bare feet! How you must have looked!"

"I s'pose I did. But, somehow, Mops, when I found myself there, it didn't seem queer at all. I just wanted to float on the red flowers."

"Kit, I do believe you're half luny," observed King; "you have the craziest ideas. But I'm jolly glad you didn't get hurt, you old sleep-trotter!" and the boy pulled his sister's curls to express his deep affection and gratitude for her safety.

Kitty was none the worse for her fall. The soft loam of the newly made flower bed had received her gently, and not even a bruise had resulted.

But the elders decided that hereafter the exits from Kitty's bedroom must be properly safeguarded at night, as no one could tell when the impulse of sleep-walking might overtake her.

There was plenty to do at Lakewood. Uncle Steve took the children for a brisk walk through the town, and bought them souvenirs of all sorts. The shops displayed tempting wares, and the girls were made happy by bead necklaces and pretty little silk bags, while King rejoiced in queer Indian relics found in a curio shop. Then back to the hotel, for a game of tennis and a romp with Cousin Jack, and in the afternoon a long motor ride, with occasional stops for ice cream soda or peanuts.

And the next day Kitty and Uncle Steve went home. They concluded to take the train from Lakewood, and not return again to Seacote.

"Grandma will be getting anxious to see us," Uncle Steve declared. "I did not intend to stay as long as this when I left home."

"Good-bye, old Kitsie," said Midget; "don't walk into any more red seas, and write to me often, won't you?"

"Yes, I will, Midge; but you don't write very often, yourself."

"I know it; it's a sort of a bother to write letters. But I love to get them."

"Well, the summer will be over pretty soon," returned Kitty, "and then we'll all be back in Rockwell."

The Maynard children were philosophical, and so they parted with cheery good-byes, and the train steamed away with Uncle Steve and Kitty waving from the window.

"Now, for our own plans," said Mr. Maynard. "What shall we do next, Jack?"

"I know what I'd like," said Cousin Ethel.

"What is it, my Angel?" asked her husband. "You may most certainly have anything you want."

"Well, instead of going right back to Seacote, I'd like to go to

Atlantic City."

"You would!" said Mr. Bryant. "And would you like to go around by Chicago, and stop at San Francisco on your way home?"

"No," said Cousin Ethel, laughing; "and I don't think Atlantic City is so very far. We could go there to-day, stay over to-morrow, and back to Seacote the day after. What do you think, Jack?"

"I think your plan is great! And I'm more than ready to carry it out, if these Maynards of ours agree to it."

"I'd like it," declared Marjorie. "I've never been to Atlantic City."

"But it isn't exactly a summer place, is it?" asked Mrs. Maynard.

"Neither is Lakewood," said Cousin Ethel. "But it's a cool spell just now, and I think it would be lots of fun to run down there."

"All right," said Mr. Maynard, "let's run."

And run they did. Considering they had nine people and two motors, and several suitcases to look after, they displayed admirable expedition in getting started, and just at dusk they came upon the brilliant radiance of the lights of Atlantic City.

"This was a fine idea of yours, Ethel," said Mrs. Maynard. "This place looks very attractive."

"Oh, isn't it!" cried Marjorie. "I think it's grand! Can't we stay up late to-night, Mother?"

"You may stay up till nine o'clock, Midget, and we'll go down and see the crowds on the Boardwalk."

So after dinner they went down to the gay thoroughfare known as the Boardwalk. It was crowded with merry, laughing, chattering people, and Midget danced along in an ecstasy of enjoyment.

"I never saw such a lot of people!" she exclaimed. "Where are they all going?"

"Nowhere in particular," said her father. "They're just out here to look at each other and enjoy themselves."

"See those funny chairs, on rollers," went on Midget. "Oh, can't we ride in them? Everybody else does."

"Of course we must," said her father. "It's part of the performance."

He engaged three rolling chairs, and as each chair held two people, he said, "How shall we divide up?"

"I'll take Mehitabel," said Cousin Jack, "and Hezekiah can go with my wife. Then you two elder Maynards can use the third. How's that?"

This arrangement was satisfactory and they started off, a strong man pushing each chair.

"Don't you think this is fun, Cousin Jack?" asked Marjorie, as she watched the crowds and the lights, and Old Ocean rolling big black waves up on the shore.

"Yes, Mehitabel, I think it's gay. There's a certain something at this place that you never see anywhere else."

"Yes, it's quite different from Seacote, isn't it? Everybody here seems to be in a hurry."

"That's only because it's such a big and lively crowd. Here we are at the pier. I think we'd better go in and hear the music."

Carolyn Wells

So they dismissed the chairmen, and went far down the long pier to listen to a concert.

A children's dance was being held, and Marjorie sat down, enraptured at the sight.

Lots of boys and girls about her own age, in fancy costumes, were dancing and pirouetting in time with the fine music. One little girl, especially, Marjorie admired. She was a pretty child, in a white frock and blue sash, and she wore a wreath of small rosebuds on her curly, flaxen hair. She seemed to be the best of all the dancers, and twice she danced alone, doing marvellous fancy steps and receiving great applause from the audience.

"Isn't she lovely!" exclaimed Midget. "I wish I could dance like that."

"You never can, Mopsy," said King. "You're too heavy. That girl is a featherweight."

"She looks nice," said Midget. "I'd like to know her."

And then, as it was nearing nine o'clock, they left the dancing pavilion, and made their way back to their hotel.

Marjorie kept close to her parents, for the crowd seemed to grow denser all the time, and if she lost sight of her people, she feared she'd be swept away from them forever.

They were staying at Madden Hall, and as they reached it, there, too, music was being played, and some people were dancing in the big ballroom. But there were no children about, so Midget trotted off to bed cheerfully, with lots of pleasant anticipations for the morrow.

At breakfast, next morning, she was looking around the dining room, when she spied the same little girl who had danced so prettily the night before.

"Oh, Mother," she exclaimed, "there she is! That pretty girl that danced. See, at the next table but two. Yes, it *is* the same one!"

"Sure it is," agreed King. "She's staying here. Perhaps we can get acquainted with her, Mops."

"Could we, Mother? Would it be right?"

"We'll see about it," said Mrs. Maynard, smiling at her impulsive daughter. After breakfast the Maynard party walked out on the veranda, and Midget soon saw the little girl, in a big rocking chair not far away.

"May I go over and speak to her, Mother?" she said.

"Why, yes, Midget, if you like. She looks like a nice child. Run along."

So Midget went over and took the next rocking chair, for there were many chairs, ranged in long rows.

"I came over to talk to you," she said; "I saw you dance last night, and I think you do dance lovely."

"Do you?" said the little girl. She seemed diffident, but pleased at Marjorie's words. "You see, it was a Children's Carnival, and Mamma let me dance. I never danced in a place like that before, and I was a little scared at first."

"You didn't look scared. You just looked lovely. What's your name? Mine's Marjorie Maynard. I live in Rockwell, when I'm home."

"Mine's Ruth Rowland, and I live in Philadelphia, when I'm home. But we're spending the summer in Seacote. We just came down here for a week."

"In Seacote! Why, that's where we're spending the summer.

We have a house on Fairway Avenue."

"Oh, I know that house. I remember seeing you there when I've passed by. Isn't it funny that we should happen to meet here! We live farther down, past the pier, you know."

"Yes, I know. Will you come to see me after we both get back there?"

"Yes, indeed I will. When are you going back?"

"To-morrow, I think. When are you?"

"In a few days. Do you know Cicely Ross?"

"No, I don't know very many children in Seacote. Do you know the Craig boys?"

"No. I guess we don't know the same people. But I know Hester Corey, and you do, too, 'cause I've seen her playing in your yard."

"Oh, yes, Hester plays with us a lot."

"She's a funny girl, isn't she?"

"Well, she's nice sometimes, and sometimes she isn't. Here's my brother King. King, this is Ruth Rowland, and what do you think? She lives in Seacote! I mean, for the summer she's staying there."

"Good!" cried King. "We can play together then, after we go back."

The three children rapidly became good friends, and soon Ruth proposed that they all go for a ride in a roller chair.

"They have wide chairs," she said, "that will hold all three of us."

Midget ran to ask her mother if they might do this, but Mrs. Maynard was not willing that the children should go alone.

"But Nannie and Rosamond may go, too, in another chair," she said, "and then I shall feel that you are looked after."

So down to the Boardwalk they went, and Nurse Nannie and Rosy Posy took one chair, and the three children took another. They selected a wide one which gave them plenty of room, and off they started.

It was a lovely, clear day, and the blue sky and the darker blue ocean met at the far distant horizon, with whitecaps dotted all over the crests of the waves. A few ships and steamers were to be seen, but mostly the children's attention was attracted to the scenes on shore.

"I thought it was lovely last night," said Midget, "but it's even nicer now. The booths and shops are so gay and festive, and the ladies all look so pretty in their summer frocks and bright parasols."

They stopped occasionally, for soda water or candy, and once they stopped at a camera place and had their pictures taken in the rolling chairs.

King proposed this, because he saw a great many people doing it, and as the man finished up the pictures at once, the children were delighted with the postcards.

"I'll send one to Kit," said Midget, "she'll love it. And I'll send one to Grandma Maynard."

Ruth had several of the pictures, too, and she said she should send some to friends in Philadelphia.

"She's an awfully nice girl," said Marjorie to her mother, when telling of their morning's doings. "I'm so glad she's at Seacote. We're going to have lots of fun when we get back."

"I'm glad, too," said Mrs. Maynard. "For you have so few acquaintances there, and Ruth is certainly a very sweet child."

CHAPTER XVII

WHAT HESTER DID

"I won't have her!" declared Hester. "I'm Queen of this Court, and I won't have any new members taken in. You had no right, Marjorie Maynard, to ask her to belong, without consulting me!"

"Why, Hester, I had so! You may be Queen, but you don't own the whole Sand Club! And Ruth Rowland is a lovely girl. How can you dislike her, when you know how sweet and pretty she is. She says she knows you."

"Yes, I do know her. Stuck-up, yellow-haired thing!"

Sand Court was in full session, and all had been going on amicably until Marjorie had chanced to mention meeting Ruth at Atlantic City, and said she had asked her to come to the Sand Club meetings. At this, Hester had flown into one of her rages, and declared that Ruth should not become a member of their little circle.

"Look here, Hester Corey," said Tom Craig, "you promised, if you could be Queen, to be always sweet and pleasant. Do you call this keeping your promise?"

"Pooh, who cares! I only promised, if the club stayed just the same. If you're going to put in a lot of new members without asking me, my promise doesn't count."

"Ruth isn't 'a lot,'" said Marjorie, laughing at Hester's fury.

But her laughter only made Queen Sandy more angry than ever.

"I don't care if she isn't! She's a new member, and I won't have *any* new members,—so, there, now!"

"Say, Hester," began King, "I don't think you're boss of this club. Just because you're Queen, you don't have any more say than the Grand Sandjandrum, or me, or anybody."

"I do, too! A Queen has *all* the say,—about everything! And I say there sha'n't be any more people in this club, and so there sha'n't!"

Hester stamped her foot and shook her fist and wagged her head in the angriest possible way, and if the others hadn't been so exasperated by her ill-temper they must have laughed at the funny picture she made. Her new crown was tumbled sideways, her hair ribbons had come off, and her face, flushed red and angry, was further disfigured by a disagreeable scowl.

And just at this moment Ruth arrived. She came in, smiling, neatly dressed in a clean print frock, and broad straw hat with a wreath of flowers round it.

"Hello, Marjorie," she said, a little shyly, for she didn't know the Craig boys, and she couldn't help seeing that Hester was in a fit of temper.

"Hello, Ruth," said Marjorie, running to her, and taking her by the hand. "Come on in; this is Sand Court. These are the Craig boys,—Tom, Dick, and Harry. And this is our Queen,—but I think you know Hester Corey."

"Yes," began Ruth, but Hester cried out: "I don't want her to know me! She sha'n't join our club, I say!"

Ruth looked bewildered at first, and then her sweet little face wrinkled up, and the tears came into her big blue eyes.

"Don't cry, Ruth," said Midget, putting her arm round her; "Hester is sort of mad this morning, but I guess she'll get over it. Don't mind her."

"I won't get over it," screamed Hester. "I'm not going to have Ruth Rowland in this club!"

"For goodness gracious sakes, children, what *is* the matter?"

A grown-up voice exclaimed these words, and then Mr. Jack Bryant entered Sand Court. He took in the situation at a glance, but pretended to be ignorant of the true state of things.

"What's up, O Queen?" he said, addressing Hester. "Oh, sunny-faced, honey-voiced Queen of Sand Court, what, I prithee, is up?"

"Nothing," growled Hester, looking sullen.

"Nay, nay, not so, sweet Queen; I bethink me there is much up, indeed! Else why these unusual consternations on the faces of thy courtiers?"

Of course, Cousin Jack knew all about the doings of Sand Court. He had often been with them, and delighted them all by talking "Court language," but to-day nobody responded to his pleasantry. Ruth and Marjorie were on the verge of tears, the boys were all angry at Hester, and Hester herself was in one of her wildest furies.

She refused to answer Cousin Jack, and sat on her throne, shrugging her shoulders and twitching about, with every cross expression possible on her pouting face. Mr. Bryant became more serious.

"Children," he said, "this won't do. This Sand Club is a jolly, good-natured club, usually, and now that I see you all at sixes and sevens, I want to know what's the matter. Midget, will you tell me?"

"I want Ruth Rowland to be in our club," said Marjorie, straightforwardly; "and Hester doesn't want her. And Hester says that because she is Queen, we must all do as she says."

"Ah, ha; urn, hum. Well, Hester, my dear child, *why* don't you want Ruth in the club?"

"Because I don't!" and the Queen looked more disagreeable than ever.

"Because you *don't*! Well, now, you see, my dear, that is just no reason at all, so Ruth can be a member, as far as you're concerned."

"No, she can't! I won't have her in!"

"Why?"

"Because I don't like her!"

"Ah, now we're getting at it. And suppose any of the club shouldn't like you; then you couldn't be a member, could you?"

"They *do* like me!" declared Hester.

"*Like* you! like *you*! A girl that flies into rages, and says unkind things? Oh, no, nobody could like a girl like that! Now, I'll fix it. You, Hester, won't have Ruth in the club, you say. Well, then if you're not in the club yourself, of course Ruth could come in. So, the rest of the club can choose which of you two girls they'd rather have, as it seems impossible to have you both. King, as the oldest, I'll ask you first. Will you choose to have Hester or Ruth in this club?"

"Ruth," said King, promptly. "She doesn't quarrel all the time."

"Next, Tom. Which do you choose?"

"Ruth," replied Tom.

"Why, Tom Craig!" cried Hester, in surprise; "you never saw that girl till to-day!"

"No, but I've seen you," he replied; "and I can tell you, Hester, I'm tired of these scraps you're always putting up! I believe we'll have better times with Ruth Rowland."

"Marjorie," Cousin Jack went on, "which girl do you choose?"

"I'd like them both," said Midget, who couldn't quite bring herself to denounce Hester entirely.

"But Hester won't have Ruth. You must choose one or the other."

"Then I choose Ruth, Cousin Jack. For Hester does make me a lot of trouble."

Midget sighed deeply, for, truly, Hester had caused strife in the club from its very beginning.

The two smaller boys voted decidedly for Ruth, and then Cousin Jack turned to Hester.

"You see," he said, but not unkindly, "the club has unanimously expressed its preference for Ruth. I don't see that you can do anything but take your hat and go home."

Hester looked at him in amazement.

"What do you mean?" she cried. "I *won't* go home! I'm Queen, and I'll stay here and *be* Queen! Ruth can go home!"

"No," said Mr. Bryant, more decidedly this time; "Ruth is not going home. You're to go home, Hester. I happen to know that the Maynard children and the Craig boys have already shown patience and unselfishness toward your tyranny and unreasonableness—now, they're not going to be imposed on any longer. I'll have a voice in this matter myself. Either you'll stay in the club and agree to have Ruth for a member also, and be pleasant and kind to her, or else you can take your hat and go home."

Mr. Bryant spoke quietly, but very firmly. He knew all the club had been through, in putting up with Hester's tantrums, and he thought it only fair that they should be relieved of this troublesome member.

"I won't have Ruth in," she repeated, but she dropped her eyes before Mr. Bryant's stern glance.

"I'm sorry, Hester, but if you won't have Ruth in, then you must go home, yourself, and I will ask you to go at once."

"All right, I'm glad to go!" and Hester pulled off her crown and threw it on the ground, and stamped on it. Then she broke in two her pretty gilt sceptre, and threw that down. She flung her hat on her head and marched out of Sand Court with angry glances at each one. She flirted her skirts and twitched her shoulders, and though she said nothing, she was as furious a little girl as can well be imagined.

Ruth was almost frightened, for she was unaccustomed to such scenes. Nor were the Maynards used to them, except as they had seen Hester in her rages now and then.

Cousin Jack looked after the child a little sadly. He was sorry that she could behave so, but he had made up his mind that Midget and King had been imposed on by Hester for a long time, and he had determined to put a stop to it. The advent of Ruth gave a good opportunity, and he availed himself of it.

A silence fell on them all. They watched Hester as she slowly went out of Sand Court.

But as she started across the lawn, she saw a garden hose with which a man had been sprinkling the grass. He had gone off and left it lying on the ground, partly turned off.

Hester picked it up, turned it on to run full force, and whirling herself quickly around pointed it straight at Ruth. In a moment the child was-soaked,—her pretty fresh dress hung limp and wet, her curls were drenched, and the swift stream of water in her face almost knocked her over.

Marjorie sprang to Ruth's side, and received a drenching herself.

King ran to Hester to take the hose from her, but she turned it full in his face and sent him sprawling to the ground.

The Craig boys were treated the same way, and when Mr. Bryant manoeuvred to get behind Hester and pinion her arms, she wheeled and sent the splashing stream all over him.

"You little vixen!" cried Cousin Jack, as, unheeding the water, he grasped her right arm.

But the child was wonderfully agile and like an eel she squirmed out of his grasp, and wielding her ungainly weapon with her left hand, she again sprayed the water on the two girls.

"You stop that, Hester Corey!" yelled King, as he scrambled to his feet, and in another moment he and Cousin Jack succeeded in getting the hose away from Hester.

"She ought to have it turned on her!" said Cousin Jack, looking at the little fury, now dancing up and down in her angry rage. "But, I don't want anything more to do with you, miss. Go home at once, and tell your mother all that has happened."

Glad to get away without further reprimand, Hester, her wrath spent now, walked slowly across the lawn and out of the gate.

"She's a terror!" Cousin Jack commented; "now forget it, kiddies, and let's go into the house and get dried out. Are you girlies much wet?"

"Not so awfully," replied Marjorie. "Mostly our hair and, oh, yes, the front of Ruth's skirt is soaked!"

"Well, we'll build a fire in the library, and hang ourselves up to dry. Come on, all you Sand boys and girls."

They went in the house, and while they dried their hair and clothes, Cousin Jack told them funny stories and made no mention of Hester or of the Sand Club.

"Now we're going to play a game," he announced, after everybody was dry, and the fire had died away to ashes. "Here are the things to play it with."

He produced what looked like some rolls of ribbon, and six pairs of scissors. But it wasn't ribbon, it was the white paper that comes rolled in with ribbon, when bought by the piece. This paper was about an inch wide and he had enough to cut six pieces, each about ten feet long.

These pieces he fastened by one end to the wainscoting with thumb tacks, and giving the other end of each piece to one of the children, he bade them stand in a row, far enough away to hold their paper strips out straight across the room.

Then, at his given signal, each one was to begin to cut, with the scissors, straight through the middle of the paper, lengthwise, the game being to cut clear to the end without tearing the paper. Of course, if carefully done, this would divide each paper into two strips of equal width.

But the game was also to see which reached the end first, and the winner was promised a prize. If the scissors inadvertently cut off either strip, the player was "out."

"Go!" cried Cousin Jack, "and strive only for the greatest speed consistent with safety. If you go too fast, you're very likely to snip off your strips; and if you go too slow, somebody else will beat you. Hurry up, Ruth, you're going evenly, but you'll never get there at that rate! Oh, hold up, Harry! if you go so fast you'll snip it off. You're terribly close to one edge, now! Ah, there you go! one strip is chopped right off. Well, never mind, my boy, stand here by me, and watch the others. What, Tom out, too? Well, well, Tom, the more haste the less speed! Careful, Midget, you'll be out in a minute. There you go! Out it is, for Mehitabel! Well, we have three still in the running. Easy does it, King! You're getting along finely. Hurry up, Ruth. You can go faster than that, and still be safe. Dick just says nothing and saws wood. That's it, Dick, slow and sure!"

Those who were "out" watched the others with breathless interest. It would have been an easy task had there been no competition. To cut a long paper into two strips is not difficult, but to cut that paper in haste, with others looking on and commenting, is more trying. The scissors seem bewitched. The paper twists and curls, and one's fingers seem to be all thumbs. King was doing well, but he gave an impatient jerk as the paper curled round his finger, and then he was out.

Dick worked steadily, and Ruth plodded slowly along.

As they neared the end at the same time the watchers grew greatly excited.

"I bet on Ruth!" cried King; "go it, Ruth! get up! g'lang there!"

"Go on, Dick," cried Marjorie. "Clk! Clk! go 'long!"

On sped the cutters, but just as it seemed as if they must finish at the same time, Dick gave a little nervous jerk at his paper, and it tore right off.

"Oh," said Midget, "you're out, Dicksie!"

And then Ruth, slowly and carefully, cut the last few inches of her paper, and held up her two strips triumphantly. She looked so sweet and happy about it that they all declared she ought to have been the winner, and Dick said, shyly: "I'm glad you won."

The prize was a shell box that Cousin Jack had brought from Atlantic City, and Ruth dimpled with pleasure as she took it.

"Thank you so much, Mr. Bryant," she said, prettily; "I never won a prize before, and I shall always keep it."

"I'm glad you won it, Ruth," said Cousin Jack, "and I want you to let it help you forget any unpleasantness of to-day. Will you forget all that happened at Sand Court, and just remember that the Maynards and the Craigs are kind and polite children, and never mind about anybody else. And come again some time, and play in Sand Court, won't you? And I'll promise you a good and pleasant time."

Ruth agreed gladly to all this, and then she went home, so happy that the memory of her pleasant hours made her almost forget Hester's rudeness.

"Now, kiddies," said Mr. Bryant, after she had gone, "I want you, too, to forget all about Hester's performance. Don't talk it over, and don't say hard things of Hester. Just forget it, and think about something nice."

"All right, Cousin Jack," said Midget, "we'll do as you say. Come on, boys, let's race down to the beach!"

The children ran away, and after a consultation with Mrs. Maynard, Mr. Bryant set out to make a call on Mrs. Corey.

His was not a pleasant task, but he felt it his duty to tell her frankly of Hester's behavior, and to say that Mr. and Mrs. Maynard couldn't allow her further to impose on their children. Mrs. Corey didn't resent this decree, but she was greatly pained at the necessity therefor.

"I don't know what to do with Hester," she said, sadly. "The child has always been subject to those ungovernable rages. I hope she will outgrow them. I feel sorry for her, for it is not really her fault. She tries to be more patient, and sometimes succeeds; then suddenly her temper breaks out at most unexpected moments."

Mr. Bryant did not say what he thought; that Hester was a spoiled child, and that had her mother taught her how sinful such a temper was, she could have learned to control it, at least, to a degree.

But he said that the Maynards could not allow Hester to come to Sand Court any more, unless with the thorough understanding and agreement that Ruth was to be a member of the Sand Club, and that Marjorie was to be Queen again. He said that Hester had forfeited all right to be Queen, and that as Midget practically formed the club, the right to be Queen was hers.

Mrs. Corey agreed to all this, expressed great chagrin that Hester had acted so rudely, and promised to talk to the child and try to induce a better spirit of kindness and good comradeship.

And Cousin Jack went away, feeling that he had served the little Maynards a good turn, if it had been a difficult and unpleasant duty to perform.

Carolyn Wells

CHAPTER XVIII

A FINE GAME

One Saturday morning, the Maynards and the Bryants sat on the veranda of "Maynard Manor," and every one of them was gazing at the sky.

"It will,—I know it will," said Mrs. Maynard, hopelessly.

"It won't,—I know it won't!" exclaimed Marjorie, smiling at her mother.

"It's bound to," declared Cousin Jack, "and there's no use thinking it won't!"

Of course, they were talking about the rain, which hadn't yet begun to fall, but which, judging from the ominous gray sky and black clouds, would soon do so.

"Yep, there are the first drops now!" cried King, as some black spots suddenly appeared on the veranda steps.

"Yep! that settles it!" Marjorie agreed, "we'll have to give up the trip. What can we do, nice, instead?"

They had planned an all-day motor trip. Mr. Maynard was always at home on Saturdays, and he liked nothing better than to take his family and friends for a ride.

"The nicest thing just now would be to scoot indoors!" said Cousin Jack, as the drops came faster and thicker, and a gust of wind sent the rain dashing at them.

So they all scurried into the house, and gathered in the big living-room to discuss the situation.

"It does seem too bad to have it rain on a Saturday," said Cousin Ethel, looking regretfully out of the window.

"Rain, rain, go away, come again another day," chanted Midget, drumming on the pane with her finger tips.

"Oh, if I were a kiddy, I shouldn't mind it," said Cousin Jack, teasingly, to Marjorie. "There are lots of things you can play. But us poor grown-ups have no fun to look forward to but motoring, and now we can't do that."

"Oh, if I were a grown-up, *I* shouldn't mind it," said Midget, laughing back at him. "Grown-ups can do anything they like, but kiddies have to do as they're told."

"Ah, yes," and Cousin Jack sighed deeply, "but we have sorrows and cares that you know nothing of."

"Yes," returned Marjorie, "and *we* have sorrows and cares that *you* know nothing of! I'd like you to change places with us for a day, and see—"

"All right, we will!" exclaimed Cousin Jack. "That's a fine game! For to-day, we grown-ups will be the children and you and King can play mother and father to us!"

"Oh, what larks!" cried King. "Let's begin right away! Will you, Mother?"

Mrs. Maynard laughed. "I'll try it," she said, "but not for all day. Say till afternoon."

"Well, till five o'clock this afternoon," suggested Marjorie; "will you, Father, will you?"

"I'll play any game the rest play," said good-natured Mr. Maynard. "What do you want me to do?"

"Well, you must obey us implicitly! King is Father, and I'm Mother, and you four are our children; Helen and Ed, and Ethel and Jack, your names are! Oh, what fun! King, what shall we do first?"

"Hear their lessons, I guess. Now, my dears, I know it's vacation, but you really ought to study a little each day, to keep your minds from rusting out."

This was a favorite speech of Mrs. Maynard's, and as King quoted it, with a twinkle in his eye, it was recognized at once, at least, by the four Maynards.

"All right," cried Marjorie, dancing about in excitement, "sit in a row, children. Why, Ed, your hands are a sight! Go at once, and wash them, my boy, and never appear before me again with such an untidy appearance!"

Mr. Maynard obediently left the room, and when he returned a few moments later, his hands were immaculately clean. Also, he was munching a cooky, apparently with great delight.

"Give me one!" demanded Cousin Jack.

"And me!" "And me!" begged both the ladies, trying to act like eager children. Mr. Maynard drew more cookies from his pockets and gave them to the others, not, however, including King and Marjorie.

"Now, children, finish your cookies, but don't drop crumbs on the floor," said Midget, choking with laughter at Cousin Jack, who was cramming large bits of his cake into his mouth.

"Please, Mother, may I go and get a drink of water?" he mumbled.

"Yes, Jack, go. And then don't ever take such big bites of cooky again! You children have the worst manners I ever saw!"

And then each one had to have a drink of water, and there was much laughter and scrambling before they were again in order for their lessons.

"Geography, first," said King, picking up a magazine to serve as a pretended text-book.

"Edward, bound Missouri."

"Missouri is bounded on the north,—by,—by,—Kansas, I guess."

"Pshaw! he doesn't know his lesson! let me say it!" exclaimed Cousin Jack. "Missouri is bounded on the north by Kentucky, on the east by Alabama, on the south by New Jersey, and on the west by Philadelphia. It is a great cotton-growing state, and contains six million inhabitants, mostly Hoosiers."

"Fine!" cried Marjorie, "every word correct! Next, Ethel, what is the Capital of the United States?"

"Seacote," said Cousin Ethel, laughing.

"Sure it is!" agreed King; "now that's enough jography. Next, we'll have arithmetic. Helen, how much is eighteen times forty-seven?"

"I don't know," said Mrs. Maynard, helplessly.

"Don't know your multiplication table! Fie, fie, my dear! You must stay in after school and study it. Edward, how much *is* eighteen times forty-seven?"

"Six hundred and fifty-nine, Father."

"Right, my boy! Go up head."

"Now, I'll give an example," said Midget. "If Edward has three eggs and Jack has two eggs, how many have they together?"

"Can't do it!" declared Cousin Jack, "'cause Ed and I are never together at breakfast, and that's the only time we have eggs!"

"Then here's another!" cried Midget; "how can you divide thirteen apples evenly among four people?"

"You can't!" said Cousin Jack, "that's the answer."

"No, it isn't! Who knows?"

"Invite in nine more people," suggested Mr. Maynard.

"No; that's not it! Oh, it's easy! Don't you know, Mother? I mean, *Helen*?"

But they all gave it up, so Marjorie announced the solution, which is, "Make apple sauce!"

"History lesson, now," said King. "Edward, who discovered America?"

"Pocahontas," replied Mr. Maynard.

"Right. Who was Pocahontas?"

"A noble Indian Princess, who was born July 29th, 1563."

"Very good. Ethel, describe the Battle of Bunker Hill."

"I can't; I wasn't there."

"You should have gone," reprimanded King, severely. "Didn't

you read the newspaper accounts of it?"

"Yes, but I didn't believe them."

"Jack Bryant, can you describe this famous battle?"

"Yes, sir. It was fought under the shadow of the Bunker Hill Monument. At sundown the shadow ceased, so they all said, 'Disperse ye rebels, and lay down your arms!' So they laid down their arms and went to sleep."

"Very well done, Master Bryant. Now, we're going to speak pieces. Each pupil will speak a piece or write a composition. You may take your choice."

"I'll speak a piece! Let me speak first!" exclaimed Cousin Ethel, jumping up and down. "May I speak now, Teacher!"

"Yes, Ethel, dear," said Midget, kindly; "you may speak your piece first. Stand up here, by me. Make your bow."

So Cousin Ethel came up to Marjorie, and acted like a very shy and bashful child. She put her finger in her mouth, and dropped her eyes and wriggled about, and picked at her skirt, until everybody was in peals of laughter.

"Be quiet, children," said Midget, trying to control her own face. "Now, everybody sit still while Ethel Bryant recites."

Cousin Ethel made a very elaborate dancing-school bow, and then, swaying back and forth in school-child fashion, she recited in a monotonous singsong, these lines:

"MUD PIES

"The grown-ups are the queerest folks; they never seem to know That mud pies always have to be made just exactly so. You have to have a nice back yard, a sunny pleasant day, And then you ask some boys and girls to come around and

play. You mix some mud up in a pail, and stir it with a
stick; It mustn't be a bit too thin—and not a bit too thick.
And then you make it into pies, and pat it with your hand,
And bake 'em on a nice flat board, and my! but they are
grand!"

Mrs. Bryant declaimed, with suitable gestures, and finally sat
down on the floor and made imaginary mud pies, in such a
dear, childish way that her audience was delighted, and gave
her really earnest encores.

"Do you know another piece, Ethel?" asked Marjorie.

"Yes, ma'am," and Mrs. Bryant resumed her shy voice and
manner.

"Then you may recite it, as your little schoolmates seem
anxious to have you do so."

So again, Mrs. Bryant diffidently made her bow, and recited,
with real dramatic effect:

   "AN UNVISITED LOCALITY

   "I wisht I was as big as men,
   To see the Town of After Ten;
   I've heard it is so bright and gay,
   It's almost like another day.
   But to my bed I'm packed off straight
   When that old clock strikes half-past eight!
   It's awful hard to be a boy
   And never know the sort of joy
   That grown-up people must have when
   They're in the Town of After Ten.
   I'm sure I don't know what they do,
   For shops are closed, and churches too.
   Perhaps with burglars they go 'round,
   And do not dare to make a sound!
   Well, soon I'll be a man, and then

I'll see the Town of After Ten!"

"Oh, Cousin Ethel, you're lovely!" cried Marjorie, forgetting her role for the moment. But King took it up.

"Yes, little Ethel," he said, "you recite very nicely, for such a young child. Now, go to your seat, and Helen Maynard may recite next."

"Mine is a Natural History Poem," said Mrs. Maynard, coming up to the teacher's desk. "It is founded on fact, and it is highly instructive."

"That's nice," said King. "Go ahead with it."

So Mrs. Maynard made her bow and though not bashful, like Mrs. Bryant, she was very funny, for she pretended to forget her lines, and stammered and hesitated, and finally burst into pretended tears. But, urged on and encouraged by the teachers, she finally concluded this gem of poesy:

"THE WHISTLING WHALE

"A whistling whale once built his nest
On the very tiptop of a mountain's crest.
He wore a tunic and a blue cocked hat,
And for fear of mice he kept a cat.
The whistling whale had a good-sized mouth,
It measured three feet from north to south;
But when he whistled he puckered it up
Till it was as small as a coffee-cup.
The people came from far and near
This wonderful whistling whale to hear;
And in a most obliging way
He stood on his tail and whistled all day."

"That's a truly noble poem," commented King, as she finished. "Take your seat, Helen; you have done splendidly, my little girl!"

Carolyn Wells

"Now, Teddy Maynard, it's your turn," said Marjorie.

"After Jacky," declared Mr. Maynard, and nothing would induce him to precede his friend.

"Mine is about a visit I paid to the Zoo," said Mr. Bryant, looking modest. "I wrote it myself for a composition, but it turned out to be poetry. I never can tell how my compositions are going to turn out."

"Recite it," said Marjorie, "and we'll see if we like it."

"It's about wild animals," went on Cousin Jack, "and it tells of their habits."

"That's very nice," said King, condescendingly; "go ahead, my boy."

So Cousin Jack recited this poem:

"THE WAYS OF THE WILD

"There's nothing quite so nice to do
As pay a visit to the zoo,
And see beasts that, at different times,
Were brought from strange and distant climes.
I love to watch the tapirs tape;
I stand intent, with mouth agape.
Then I observe the vipers vipe;
They're a most interesting type.
I love to see the beavers beave;
Indeed, you scarcely would believe
That they can beave so cleverly,
Almost as well as you or me.
And then I pass along, and lo!
Panthers are panthing to and fro.
And in the next cage I can see
The badgers badging merrily.
Oh, the dear beasties at the zoo,

What entertaining things they do!"

"That's fine!" exclaimed Midget. "I didn't know we were going to have a *real* entertainment!"

"Very good, Jacky!" pronounced King. "I shall mark you ten in declamation. You're a good declaimer. Now, Teddy Maynard, it's your turn."

"Mine is real oratory," declared Mr. Maynard, as he rose from his seat. "But I find that so many fine oratorical pieces fizzle out after their first lines, that I just pick out the best lines and use them for declamation. Now, you can see how well my plan works."

He struck an attitude, bowed to each of his audience separately, cleared his throat impressively, and then began to declaim in a stilted, stagey voice, and with absurd dramatic gestures:

"THE ART OF ELOCUTION

"The noble songs of noble deeds of bravery or glory
Are much enhanced if they're declaimed with stirring oratory.
I love sonorous words that roll like billows o'er the seas;
These I recite like Cicero or like Demosthenes.

"And so, from every poem what is worthy I select;
I use the phrases I like best, the others I reject;
And thus, I claim, that I have found the logical solution
Of difficulties that attend the art of elocution.

"Whence come these shrieks so wild and shrill? Across the sands o' Dee?
Lo, I will stand at thy right hand and keep the bridge with thee!
For this was Tell a hero? For this did Gessler die?

'The curse is come upon me!' said the Spider to the Fly.
"When Britain first at Heaven's command said, 'Boatswain, do not tarry;
The despot's heel is on thy shore, and while ye may, go marry.'
Let dogs delight to bark and bite the British Grenadiers,
Lars Porsena of Clusium lay dying in Algiers!

"Old Grimes is dead! Ring out, wild bells! And shall Trelawney die?
Then twenty thousand Cornishmen are comin' thro' the rye!
The Blessed Damozel leaned out,—she was eight years old *she said!*
Lord Lovel stood at his castle gate, whence all but him had fled.

"Rise up, rise up, Xarifa! Only three grains of corn!
Stay, Lady, stay! for mercy's sake! and wind the bugle horn.
The glittering knife descends—descends—Hark, hark, the foeman's cry!
The world is all a fleeting show! Said Gilpin, 'So am I!'

"The sea! the sea! the open sea! Roll on, roll on, thou deep!
Maxwelton braes are bonny, but Macbeth hath murdered sleep!
Answer me, burning shades of night! what's Hecuba to me?
Alone stood brave Horatius! The boy—oh, where was he?"

"Oh, Father!" cried Marjorie, as Mr. Maynard finished, "did you really make that up? Or did you find it in a book?"

But Mr. Maynard wouldn't tell, and only accepted the praise heaped upon him, with a foolish smirk, like an embarrassed schoolboy.

"Now, children, school is out," said Midget, "and it's about luncheon time. So go and tidy yourselves up to come to the table. You're always sending us to tidy up, Mother, so now you can see what a nuisance it is! Run along, and come back as quickly as you can, for luncheon is nearly ready."

The four grown-ups went away to tidy up, and King and Midget made further plans for this new game. It was still raining, so there was no hope of going motoring, and they concluded they were having enough fun at home to make up for it.

But when the four "children" returned, they looked at them a moment in silent astonishment, and then burst into shrieks of laughter.

Mr. Maynard and Mr. Bryant had transformed themselves into boys, by brushing their hair down very wet and straight, and wearing large, round collars made of white paper, and tied with enormous bows. They looked funny enough, but the two ladies were funnier still. Mrs. Maynard had her hair in two long pigtails tied with huge ribbons, and Cousin Ethel had her hair in bunches of curls, also tied with big bows. They both wore white bib aprons, and carried foolish-looking dolls which they had made out of pillows, tied round with string.

"You *dear* children!" cried Midget; "I think you are lovely! Come along to luncheon."

The "children" politely let King and Midget go first, and they followed, giggling. Sarah, the waitress, was overcome with amusement, but she managed to keep a straight face, as the comical-looking procession filed in.

King and Marjorie appropriated their parents' seats, and the others sat at the sides of the table.

"No, Helen, dear," said Midget, "you can't have any tea. It isn't good for little girls. You may have a glass of milk, if you wish."

"I don't think these lobster croquettes are good for Jack," said

King, looking wisely at Midget; "they're very rich, and he's subject to indigestion."

"I am not!" declared Cousin Jack, looking longingly at the tempting croquettes, for which Ellen was famous.

"There, there, my child," said Marjorie; "don't contradict your father. Perhaps he could have a half of one, King."

"Yes, that would scarcely make him ill," and King gave Cousin Jack a portion of one small croquette, which he ate up at once, and found to be merely an aggravation.

"Oh, no! no pie for Edward," said Marjorie, when a delicious lemon meringue made its appearance. "Pie is entirely unsuitable for children! He may have a nice baked apple."

And Mr. Maynard was plucky enough to eat his baked apple without a murmur, for he remembered that often he had advised Mrs. Maynard against giving the children pie.

To be sure, the pie would not harm the grown people, but Mr. Maynard had agreed to "play the game," and it was his nature to do thoroughly whatever he undertook.

CHAPTER XIX

MORE FUN

"Now, Helen," said Marjorie, as they left the dining-room, "you must practise for an hour."

"Oh, Mother, I don't feel a bit like it! Mayn't I skip it to-day?"

This was, in effect, a speech that Marjorie often made, and she had to laugh at her mother's mimicry.

But she straightened her face, and said, "No, my child; you must do your practising, or you won't be ready for your lesson when the teacher comes to-morrow."

"All right, Mother," said Mrs. Maynard, cheerfully, and sitting down at the piano, she began to rattle off a gay waltz.

"Oh, no, Helen," remonstrated Marjorie, "that won't do! You must play your scales and exercises. See, here's the book. Now, play that page over and over for an hour."

Marjorie did hate those tedious "exercises," and she was glad for her mother to see how poky it was to drum at them for an hour. As a rule, Marjorie did her practising patiently enough, but sometimes she revolted, and it made her chuckle to see Mrs. Maynard carefully picking out the "five-finger drills."

"Keep your hands straight, Helen," she admonished her

Carolyn Wells

mother. "Keep the backs of them so level that a lead pencil wouldn't roll off. I'll get a lead pencil."

"No, don't!" exclaimed Mrs. Maynard, in dismay. She liked to play the piano, but she was far from careful to hold her hands in the position required by Midget's teacher.

"Yes, I think I'd better, Helen. If you contract bad habits, it's so difficult to break them."

Roguish Marjorie brought a lead pencil, and laid it carefully across the back of her mother's hand, from which it immediately rolled off.

"Now, Helen, you must hold your hand level. Try again, dearie, and if it rolls off, pick it up and put it back in place."

Mrs. Maynard made a wry face, and the other grown-ups laughed, to see the difficulty she experienced with the pencil.

"One—two—three—four," she counted, aloud.

"Count to yourself, Helen," said Marjorie. "It's annoying to hear you do that!"

This, too, was quoted, for Mrs. Maynard had often objected to the monotonous drone of Marjorie's counting aloud.

But the mother began to see that a child's life has its own little troubles, and she smiled appreciatively at Midget, as she picked up the pencil from the floor for the twentieth time, and replaced it on the back of her hand, now stiff and lame from the unwonted restraint.

"You dear old darling!" cried Midget, flying over and kissing the patient musician; "you sha'n't do that any longer! I declare, King, it's clearing off, after all! Let's take the children out for a walk."

"Very well, we will. Oh, here comes Ruth! Come in, Ruth."

Ruth Rowland came in, and looked greatly mystified at the appearance of the elder members of the group before her.

But King and Midget explained what was going on, and said:

"And you can be Aunt Ruth, come to call on us and our children."

Ruth's eyes danced with fun, and she sat down, saying to Marjorie, "I'm glad to see the children looking so well; have any of them the whooping-cough? I hear it's around some."

"I have," declared Cousin Jack, and then he began to cough and whoop in a most exaggerated imitation of the whooping-cough. Indeed, in his paroxysms, he almost turned somersaults.

"I hab a bad cold id by head," declared Mr. Maynard, and he began a series of such prodigious sneezes that all the others screamed with laughter.

"Well, your children aren't so very well, after all, are they?" commented Ruth, as they watched the two men cutting up their capers.

"The girls are," said Marjorie, looking affectionately at her two "daughters."

"Oh, I'm not!" declared Mrs. Maynard; "I have a fearful toothache," and she held her cheek in her hand, and rocked back and forth, pretending dreadful pain.

"And I have the mumps!" announced Cousin Ethel, puffing out her pretty pink cheeks, to make believe they were swollen with that ailment.

"Well, you're a crowd of invalids!" said King; "I believe some fresh air would do you good. Out you all go, for a walk. Get your hats, kiddies, and be quick about it."

The grown-ups scampered away to get their hats, and the ladies put up their hair properly and took off their white aprons.

The two men discarded their big collars and ties, but the game was not yet over, and the group went gayly out and down toward the beach.

"May we go in bathing, Mother?" asked Mr. Maynard.

"Not in bathing, my son," returned Marjorie; "the waves are too strong. But, if you wish, you may all take off your shoes and stockings and go 'paddling.'"

However, none of the quartette of "children" accepted this permission, so they all sat on the sand and built forts.

"Now, I guess we'll all go to the pier, and get ice cream," said King. "How would you like that, kiddies?"

"Fine!" said Cousin Jack. "It's getting warmer, and I'm hungering for ice cream. Come on, all."

"Gently, my boy, gently," said King, as Cousin Jack scrambled to his feet, upsetting sand all over everybody. "Now, walk along nicely and properly, don't go too fast, and we'll reach the pier in good time."

"Turn out your toes," directed Marjorie; "hold up your head, Ethel. Don't swing your arms, Edward."

As a matter of fact the four grown people found it a little difficult to follow these bits of good advice they had so often given carelessly to the children, and they marched along rather stiffly.

"Try to be a little more graceful, Helen," said King, and they all laughed, for Mrs. Maynard was really a very graceful lady, and was spoiling her gait by over-attention to Midget's rules. At the pier, King selected a pleasant table, and ranged his party around it.

"Bring three plates of ice cream, and four half-portions," he directed the waiter. And when it was brought, he calmly gave the four small pieces to his parents and the Bryants.

Cousin Jack's face fell, for he was warm and tired, and he wanted more than a spoonful of the refreshing delicacy. But a surreptitious glance at his watch showed him it was almost five o'clock; so he accepted his plate without a murmur.

"It's very nice, Mother," he said demurely, eating it by tiny bits, scraped from the edges as he had sometimes seen Marjorie do, when her share had been limited to half a plate.

"I'm glad you like it, son," she returned; "don't eat too fast, —hold your spoon properly,—take small bites of cake."

Ruth was convulsed by this new sort of fun, and asked Marjorie if they had ever played the game before.

"No," Cousin Jack answered for her, "and I'm jolly well sure we never will again! I've had enough of being 'a child again, just for to-night!' And, if you please, ladies and gentlemen, it's now five o'clock! the jig is up! the game is played out! the ball is over! Here, waiter; bring some ice cream, please. Full-sized plates, all around!"

The amused waiter hurried away on his errand, and Mr. and Mrs. Maynard sat up suddenly, as if relieved of a great responsibility.

"Bring some cake, too," said Mrs. Maynard, "and a pot of tea. Don't you want some tea, Ethel?"

"Indeed, I do, Helen; I'm exhausted. Jack, if you ever propose such a game again!"

"I didn't propose it, my dear! Now, will you look at that! Everything always gets blamed on me!"

And now there was plenty of ice cream for everybody, and the children were allowed to have all they wanted, and they were all glad to get back to their rightful places again.

"But it was fun!" said Marjorie, and then she told Ruth all about the funny things they had done before she arrived on the scene.

Then they all walked around by Ruth's house to take her home, and then they walked around by Bryant Bower to take the Bryants home, and then the Maynards went home themselves.

"I'm going to write Kit all about it," said Marjorie; "she'd have loved that game, if she'd been here."

"She loves any make-believe game," said King. "You write to her, Midget; I've got to write up *The Jolly Sandboy* paper."

"I should think you had! You haven't done one for two weeks."

"I know it; but it's because nobody sends in any contributions. I can't make it all up alone."

"'Course you can't. When I write to Kitty, I'll ask her if she hasn't some things we could put in it. She and Uncle Steve are always making up poetry and stories."

"Good idea, Mops! Tell her to be *sure* to send me a lot of stuff, first thing she does!"

"Well, I will;" and Marjorie set to work at her letter.

It was finished by dinner time, for Marjorie's letters to her sister were not marked by any undue precision of style or penmanship, and as Marjorie laid it on the hall table to be mailed, she told King that she had given Kitty his message.

"Father," said Midget, at dinner, that night, "what day did Cousin Jack say was Pocahontas' birthday?"

"I don't remember, my dear; but I'm quite sure he doesn't really know, nor any one else. I fancy he made up that date."

"Well, do you know of anybody, anybody nice and celebrated, whose birthday comes about now?"

"The latter part of July? No, Midget, I don't. Why?"

"Oh, 'cause I think it would be nice to have a celebration, and you can't celebrate without a hero."

"Do you call Pocahontas a hero?" asked King, quizzically.

"Well, she's a heroine,—it's all the same. When do you s'pose her birthday was, Father?"

"I've no idea, Midget; and Cousin Jack hasn't, either. But if you want to celebrate her, you can choose any day. You see, it isn't like a birthday that's celebrated every year, Washington's, Lincoln's, or yours. If you're just going to celebrate once, you can take one day as well as another."

"Oh, can I, Father? Then, we'll have it next week. I'll choose August first,—that's a nice day."

"What's it all about, Midge?" asked King.

"Oh, nothing; only I took a notion for a celebration. We had such good times on Fourth of July and on my birthday, I want another birthday."

"I think it's a good idea to choose some uncelebrated person like Pocahontas," said Mrs. Maynard; "for if you don't celebrate her I doubt if anybody ever will."

"And you see we can have it all sort of Indian," went on Midget. "You know we've a good many Indian baskets and beads and things,—and, Father, couldn't you build us a wigwam?"

"Oh, yes, a whole reservation, if you like."

"No, just one wigwam. And we'll only have the Sand Club. I don't mean to have a party."

"All right, I'm in for it," declared King, and right after dinner, the two set to work making plans for the celebration.

"Cousin Jack will help, I know," said Marjorie; "remember how he played Indians with us, up in Cambridge, last year?"

"Yep, 'course I do. He'll be fine! He always is."

"Let's telephone, and ask him right away."

"All right;" and in a few moments Cousin Jack's cheery "Hello!" came over the wire.

"Well!" he exclaimed, "if it isn't those Maynard scamps again! Now, see here, Mehitabel, it's time you and Hezekiah went to bed. It's nearly nine o'clock."

"But, Cousin Jack, I just want to ask you something."

"Not to-night, my Angel Child. Whatever you ask me to-night, I shall say no to! Besides, I'm reading my paper, and I can't be disturbed."

"But, Cousin Jack—"

"The Interstate Commerce Commission has to-day handed down a decision in favor of—"

"Oh, King, he's reading out of his newspaper, just to tease us! You try him."

King took the telephone. "Please, Cousin Jack, listen a minute," he said.

But all the reply he heard was:

"Ephraim Hardenburg has been elected chairman of the executive committee of the Great Coal Tar Company, to succeed James H.—"

King hung up the receiver in disgust.

"No use," he said; "Cousin Jack just read more of that newspaper stuff! Never mind, Midget, we can wait till we see him. I guess I will scoot to bed, now; I'm awful sleepy."

But when Cousin Jack heard of their project, a day or two later, he was more than willing to help with the celebration.

"Well, I just guess!" he cried. "We'll have a jamboree that'll make all the good Indians wish they were alive now, instead of four hundred thousand years ago! We'll have a wigwam and a wampum and a tomahawk and all the ancient improvements! Hooray for Pocahontas!"

"Gracious, Jack! you're the biggest child of the lot!" exclaimed Mrs. Maynard, who sat on the veranda, watching the enthusiasm going on.

"Of course, I am, ma'am! I'm having a merry playtime this summer with my little friends, and as I have to work hard all winter, I really need this vacation."

"Of course you do! But don't let those two energetic children wear you out."

"No, ma'am! More likely I'll wear them out. Now, for the wigwam, kiddies. Have you a couple of Navajo blankets?"

"Yes, we have! and a Bulgarian one, or whatever you call it, to piece out," cried Midget, as she ran to get them.

"Just the thing!" declared Cousin Jack. "Put them aside, we won't use them till the day of the show. 'Cause why? 'Cause it *might* rain,—but, of course it won't. Now, for feathers,—we want lots of feathers."

"Old hat feathers?" asked Midget.

"Ostrich plumes? Nay, nay, me child. Good stiff quill feathers,—turkey feathers preferred. Well, never mind those,—I'll fish some up from somewhere. Now, blankets for the braves and fringed gowns for the squaws. I'll show you how, Mehitabel, and you and your respected mother can do the sewing act."

Well, Cousin Jack planned just about everything, and he and the children turned the house upside down in their quest for materials. But Mrs. Maynard didn't mind. She was used to it, for the Maynard children would always rather "celebrate" than play any ordinary game.

CHAPTER XX

A CELEBRATION

The first of August was a perfect day for their celebration.

They had concluded to hold a Sand Court session first, for the simple reason that so much matter for *The Jolly Sandboy* had arrived from Kitty that King said his paper was full, and he thought it would be nice to help along the celebration.

Cousin Jack declined an invitation to be present at the reading, saying that the Pocahontas part was all he could stand, so the Court convened without him. Ruth was Queen for the day. This was for no particular reason, except that Marjorie thought it would be a pleasure to the little new member, so she insisted on Ruth's wearing the crown.

Very dainty and sweet the little Queen looked, with her long flaxen curls hanging down from the extra gorgeous gilt-paper crown, that Marjorie had made specially for this occasion.

As the session began, a meek little figure appeared at the Court entrance, and there was Hester!

"Now, you Hester!" began Tom Craig, but Hester said:

"Oh, please let me come! I *will* be good. I won't say a single cross word, or boss, or anything."

"All right, Hester," said Midget, kindly, "come on in. If the Queen says you may we'll all say so. Do you, O Queen?"

Ruth looked doubtful for a minute, for she was a little afraid of Hester's uncertain temper; but, seeing Marjorie's pleading look, she consented.

"All right," she said; "if Hester won't throw water on me."

"No, I won't!" declared Hester, earnestly.

"Well," said King, "just as long as Hester behaves herself she may stay. If she carries on like fury, she's got to go home."

Hester sat down and folded her hands in her lap, looking so excessively meek that they all had to laugh at her.

"Now," said the Queen, "we're gathered here together, my loyal subjects, to listen to,—to, what do you call it?"

"*The Jolly Sandboy*," prompted King.

"*The Jolly Sandbag*," said the Queen, misunderstanding.

But she was soon put right, and King proceeded to read his paper.

"It's 'most all done by Uncle Steve and Kitty," he said, "and it's so nice, I thought you'd all like to hear it."

"We would," they said, and so King began.

"Uncle Steve's part is all about animals," he said. "It's a sort of Natural History, I guess. First is a poem about the Camel.

"The camel is a curious beast;
He roams about all through the East.
He swiftly scours the desert plain,
And then he scours it back again.

"The camel's legs are very slim,
And he lets people ride on him.
Across the sandy waste he flies,
And kicks the waste in people's eyes.

"He kneels for people to get on,
Then pulls his legs up, one by one;
But here's what troubles them the worst—
To know which leg he'll pull up first.

"Sometimes, when he is feeling gay,
The camel likes to run away;
And, as he's just indulged that whim,
I can't write any more of him."

"I think that's lovely," said the Queen, enthusiastically. "Your uncle is a real poet, isn't he?"

"Our family all can write poetry," said Marjorie, seriously. "Father and Mother both write beautiful verses."

"Now, here's the next one," went on King. "This is about all sorts of different animals,—and it's funny, too:

"The whale is smooth, and black as jet
His disposition sweet;
He neatly combs his hair, and yet
He will not wipe his feet.

"The wombat's clever and polite,
And kind as he can be;
And yet he doesn't bow quite right
When he goes out to tea.

"The snake is bright and understands
Whatever he is taught;
And yet he never will shake hands
As cordial people ought.

"'Most everybody loves the newt;
  But I've heard people tell,
  That though he's handy with a flute
  He can't sew very well.

"So animals, as you may see,
  Some grave defects display;
  They're not like human beings. We
  Are perfect every way."

"Oh, that's a fine one!" cried Hester. "Mayn't I copy that, and have it to keep?"

"Of course," said King. "I'll make you a copy on the typewriter. Now, here's a silly one. I mean nonsensical, you know. But I like it:

"THE FUNNY FLAPDOODLE

"There was a Flapdoodle of France,
  Who loved to cut capers and dance;
  He had one red shoe
  And the other was blue,
  And how he could shuffle and prance!

"One day he was kicking so high
  That a breeze blew him up in the sky;
  The breeze was so strong
  It blew him along
  Till the Flapdoodle just seemed to fly.

"He flew 'way up into the stars,
  And, somehow, he landed on Mars.
  Said the Flapdoodle: 'I
  Do not like to fly;
  I think I'll go back on the cars.'

"So a railroad was rapidly built,
  And they wrapped him all up in a quilt;

For the Flapdoodle said:
'If I stick out my head
I fear that I'll somehow get kilt!'

"The railroad train whizzed very fast,
But they landed him safely at last;
And through future years
He related, with tears,
The dangers through which he had passed."

"Oh, that's the best of all!" said Midget; "I love that kind of funny verses. Isn't Uncle Steve clever to write like that! Any more, King?"

"Yes, one more. It isn't about animals, but it's a sort of a nonsense poem, too. It's called 'A Queer Hospital.'

"There's a hospital down on Absurdity Square,
Where the queerest of patients are tended with care.

"When I made them a visit I saw in a crib
A little Umbrella who had broken his rib.

"And then I observed in the very next bed
A bright little Pin who had bumped his poor head.

"They said a new cure they'd decided to try
On an old Needle, totally blind in one eye.

"I was much interested, and soon I espied
A Shoe who complained of a stitch in her side.

"And a sad-looking patient who seemed in the dumps
Was a Clock, with a swell face because of the mumps.

"Then I tried very hard, though I fear 'twas in vain
To comfort a Window who had a bad pane.

"And I paused just a moment to cheerily speak

With a pale Cup of Tea who was awfully weak.

"As I took my departure I met on the stair
A new patient, whom they were handling with care,
A victim perhaps of some terrible wreck—
'Twas a Squash who had fatally broken his neck."

"This is the nicest *Jolly Sandboy* paper we've had yet," said Tom, as King finished.

"Yes, it is," agreed Marjorie. "But I thought Kit wrote some of it, King."

"She did. I'll read hers now. It's an alphabet, all about us down here. Kitty wrote it, but she says Uncle Steve helped her a little bit with some of the lines. It's called 'The Seacote Alphabet.'

"A is the Automobile we all love.
B is the Boat in the water we shove.
C is the Coast that stretches along.
D is for Dick, our Sandow so strong.
E's cousin Ethel, so sweet and refined.
F, Father Maynard, indulgent and kind.
G, Grandma Sherwood, who dresses in drab.
H is for Hester and Harry Sand Crab.
I, for Ice Cream, the Maynards' mainstay.
J, Cousin Jack, always ready to play.
K is for King, and for Kitty, (that's me).
L is for Lakewood, where I went to sea.
M, Mother Maynard, and Marjorie, too.
N for Nurse Nannie, who has lots to do.
O for the Ocean, with big breakers bold.
P for the Pier, where candy is sold.
Q for Queen Sandy, in regal array.
R, Rosy Posy, so dainty and gay.
S is for Seacote, and Sand Court beside.
T is for Tom, the trusty and tried.
U, Uncle Steve, who's helping me write.
V for these Verses we send you to-night.

W, the Waves, that dash with such fuss.
X the Excitement when one catches us.
Y for You Youngsters, I've given your names.
Z is the Zeal you show in your games."

"My! isn't that scrumptious!" exclaimed Hester. "You're a terribly smart family, Marjorie."

"Oh, I don't know," said Midget, modestly. "Kit's pretty clever at writing rhymes, but King and I can't do it much. We make up songs sometimes, but Kitty makes the best ones."

"I wish I could do it," said Ruth; "but I couldn't write a rhyming thing at all."

"Well, that's all there is in *The Jolly Sandboy* this week," said King. "I didn't write any myself, and the things you others gave me, I've saved for next week. Now, shall we go and celebrate Pocahontas' birthday?"

"Is it really her birthday?" asked Ruth.

"No, we're just pretending it is. But you see, poor Poky never had her birthday celebrated; I mean,—not legally, like Washington,—so we're going to give her a chance."

The Sand Club trooped up to the house, and found Cousin Jack waiting for them. He was a little surprised to see Hester, but he greeted her pleasantly, and Hester looked so meek and mild, one would hardly believe she had a high temper at all. A wigwam had been built on the lawn, and though it was only a few poles covered with blankets, it looked very Indian and effective.

The Maynards had contrived costumes for all, and in a few moments the girls had on gay-fringed skirts and little shawls, with gaudy headdresses, and the boys had a nondescript Indian garb, and wonderful feathered headpieces, that hung grandly down their backs like Big Chiefs.

Also they had pasteboard tomahawks, and Cousin Jack taught them a war-whoop that was truly ear-splitting.

"First," said Mr. Bryant, "we'll all sing the Blue Juniata, as that is a pretty Indian song, and so, sort of appropriate to Pocahontas."

So they all sang it, with a will, and the song of "The Indian Girl, Bright Alfarata," was, in a way, a tribute to Pocahontas.

"Now," Mr. Bryant went on, "some one must tell the story of Pocahontas. Harry, will you do it?"

But the Sand Crab was too shy to speak in public, so Cousin Jack asked Ruth to do it.

"I don't know it very well," said Ruth, "but I guess it was like this: Captain John Smith was about to be tommyhawked all to pieces by admiring Indians. As the fell blows were about to fell, up rushes a beautiful Indian maiden, with her black hair streaming in the breeze. 'Fear thou not!' she said, wildly; 'I will save thee!' Whereupon she flang herself upon him, and hugged him till he couldn't be reached by his tormentors. The wild Indians were forced to desist, or else pierce to the heart their own Pocahontas, beloved daughter of their tribe. So they released Captain John Smith, and so Pocahontas married Captain John Rolfe instead, and they lived happy ever after. Hence is why we celebrate her birthday."

Ruth clearly enjoyed the telling of this tale, and threw herself into it with dramatic fervor.

The others listened, enthralled by her graphic recital and thrilling diction.

"My!" exclaimed Midget, as she finished, "I didn't know you knew so many big words, Ruth."

"I didn't, either," said Ruth, calmly; "they sort of came to me as I went along."

"Well, that's just as smart as writing poetry," declared King, and Ruth was greatly pleased at the compliments.

"Now, my dear young friends," Cousin Jack said, by way of a speech, "the exercises will now begin. As you know, we are celebrating the birthday of a noble Indian Princess. Therefore, our sports or diversions will all be of an Indian character. First, we will have an Indian Club Drill."

He produced Indian clubs for all, the boys' being heavier ones than the girls.

These were new to the Maynards, but Cousin Jack soon taught them how to use them, and instructed them in a simple drill.

Hester learned more quickly than Marjorie, for she was more lithe and agile, and swung her clubs around with greater ease. Ruth seemed to know instinctively how to use them, which was partly due to her proficiency in fancy dancing. But they all learned, and greatly enjoyed the interesting exercise.

Cousin Jack presented the children with the clubs they used, and they promised to practise with them often.

"It'll be good for you growing young people," said Mr. Maynard, "and you can form a sort of a Pocahontas Club."

Then he had a gramophone brought out to the lawn, and they whisked their clubs about to inspiriting Indian music.

"Now, I dare say you're tired," said Cousin Jack, "for Indian club exercise is a strain on the muscles. So sit in a circle on the grass, and we'll all smoke pipes of peace and swap stories for a while."

The "pipes of peace" turned out to be pipes made of chocolate, so they were all willing to "smoke" them.

"Mine's a pipe of pieces!" said Midget, as she broke the stem in bits, and ate them one by one.

The others followed her example, and the pipes had disappeared before the story-telling fairly began.

But Cousin Jack told them some thrilling Indian tales, and so interested were his hearers that they gathered close about him, and listened in absorbed silence.

"Was that true, Cousin Jack?" asked King, after an exciting yarn.

"Well, it's in a story-book written by James Fenimore Cooper. You're old enough to read his books now, and if I were you children, I'd ask my parents to buy me some of Cooper's works."

"I'm going to do that," cried Hester, her eyes dancing at the thought of reading such stories for herself. "I never heard of them before."

"Well, you're young yet to read novels, but Cooper's are all right for you. You might read one aloud in your Sand Club."

"Yes, we will!" said King. "That'll be fine. Then one book would do for us all. Or we might each get one, and then lend them around to each other. My, we're getting lots of new ideas from our celebration. Indian club exercises and Cooper's stories are worth knowing about."

"And now," said Cousin Jack, "if you're rested, suppose we march along Indian File, and see if we can come across an Indian Meal."

"Ho, ho!" laughed King, "I don't want to eat Indian meal!"

"We'll see what it is before we decide," said Midget, judicially. "What is Indian File, Cousin Jack?"

"Oh, that only means single file, or one by one. *Not* like the Irishman who said to his men, 'March togither, men! be twos as far as ye go, an' thin be wans!' I want you to go 'be wans' all the way."

So, in single file, they followed Cousin Jack's lead to the wigwam, which they hadn't yet entered. He turned back the flap of the tent, and there was room for all inside. On a table there there were eight Indian baskets, of pretty design. On lifting the covers, each was found to contain an "Indian Meal."

The meal was a few dainty little sandwiches and cakes, and a peach and a pear, all wrapped in pretty paper napkins, with an Indian's head on the corner.

Exercise had given the children good appetites, and they were quite ready to do full justice to the "Indian Meal."

Sarah brought out lemonade, and later ice cream, so, as Midget said, it really was a party after all.

Of course, the children kept the baskets and the pretty napkins as souvenirs, and when the guests went home, they said they were glad they didn't know the real date of Pocahontas' birthday, for it *might* have been in the winter, and then they couldn't have had nearly as much fun.

"And it's lucky we decided on this day," said Cousin Jack, after the children had gone, "for to-morrow Ethel and I go back to Cambridge."

"Oh, Cousin Jack, not really!" cried Midget, in dismay.

"Yes, kiddy; we've changed our summer plans suddenly, and we're going to Europe next week. So we leave here to-morrow. And sorry, indeed, are we to leave our Maynard friends."

"I'm sorry, too," said Midget, "*awfully* sorry, but I'm glad we've had you down here as long as we have. You've been awful good to us, Cousin Jack."

"You've been good to me, Mehitabel. And when I wander through the interesting places abroad, I shall write letters to you, and when I come home again, I'll bring you a souvenir from every place I've been to."

"Well, you're just the dearest Cousin Jack in all the world!" said Midget, and she gave him a big hug and kiss to corroborate her words.

"And you're just the dearest Mopsy Midget Mehitabel!" he said, returning her caress.

*   *   *   *   *

Choose from Thousands of 1stWorldLibrary Classics By

A. M. Barnard
Ada Leverson
Adolphus William Ward
Aesop
Agatha Christie
Alexander Aaronsohn
Alexander Kielland
Alexandre Dumas
Alfred Gatty
Alfred Ollivant
Alice Duer Miller
Alice Turner Curtis
Alice Dunbar
Allen Chapman
Alleyne Ireland
Ambrose Bierce
Amelia E. Barr
Amory H. Bradford
Andrew Lang
Andrew McFarland Davis
Andy Adams
Angela Brazil
Anna Alice Chapin
Anna Sewell
Annie Besant
Annie Hamilton Donnell
Annie Payson Call
Annie Roe Carr
Annonaymous
Anton Chekhov
Archibald Lee Fletcher
Arnold Bennett
Arthur C. Benson
Arthur Conan Doyle
Arthur M. Winfield
Arthur Ransome
Arthur Schnitzler
Arthur Train
Atticus
B.H. Baden-Powell
B. M. Bower
B. C. Chatterjee
Baroness Emmuska Orczy
Baroness Orczy
Basil King
Bayard Taylor
Ben Macomber
Bertha Muzzy Bower
Bjornstjerne Bjornson

Booth Tarkington
Boyd Cable
Bram Stoker
C. Collodi
C. E. Orr
C. M. Ingleby
Carolyn Wells
Catherine Parr Traill
Charles A. Eastman
Charles Amory Beach
Charles Dickens
Charles Dudley Warner
Charles Farrar Browne
Charles Ives
Charles Kingsley
Charles Klein
Charles Hanson Towne
Charles Lathrop Pack
Charles Romyn Dake
Charles Whibley
Charles Willing Beale
Charlotte M. Braeme
Charlotte M. Yonge
Charlotte Perkins Stetson
Clair W. Hayes
Clarence Day Jr.
Clarence E. Mulford
Clemence Housman
Confucius
Coningsby Dawson
Cornelis DeWitt Wilcox
Cyril Burleigh
D. H. Lawrence
Daniel Defoe
David Garnett
Dinah Craik
Don Carlos Janes
Donald Keyhoe
Dorothy Kilner
Dougan Clark
Douglas Fairbanks
E. Nesbit
E. P. Roe
E. Phillips Oppenheim
E. S. Brooks
Earl Barnes
Edgar Rice Burroughs
Edith Van Dyne
Edith Wharton

Edward Everett Hale
Edward J. O'Biren
Edward S. Ellis
Edwin L. Arnold
Eleanor Atkins
Eleanor Hallowell Abbott
Eliot Gregory
Elizabeth Gaskell
Elizabeth McCracken
Elizabeth Von Arnim
Ellem Key
Emerson Hough
Emilie F. Carlen
Emily Bronte
Emily Dickinson
Enid Bagnold
Enilor Macartney Lane
Erasmus W. Jones
Ernie Howard Pie
Ethel May Dell
Ethel Turner
Ethel Watts Mumford
Eugene Sue
Eugenie Foa
Eugene Wood
Eustace Hale Ball
Evelyn Everett-green
Everard Cotes
F. H. Cheley
F. J. Cross
F. Marion Crawford
Fannie E. Newberry
Federick Austin Ogg
Ferdinand Ossendowski
Fergus Hume
Florence A. Kilpatrick
Fremont B. Deering
Francis Bacon
Francis Darwin
Frances Hodgson Burnett
Frances Parkinson Keyes
Frank Gee Patchin
Frank Harris
Frank Jewett Mather
Frank L. Packard
Frank V. Webster
Frederic Stewart Isham
Frederick Trevor Hill
Frederick Winslow Taylor

Friedrich Kerst
Friedrich Nietzsche
Fyodor Dostoyevsky
G.A. Henty
G.K. Chesterton
Gabrielle E. Jackson
Garrett P. Serviss
Gaston Leroux
George A. Warren
George Ade
Geroge Bernard Shaw
George Cary Eggleston
George Durston
George Ebers
George Eliot
George Gissing
George MacDonald
George Meredith
George Orwell
George Sylvester Viereck
George Tucker
George W. Cable
George Wharton James
Gertrude Atherton
Gordon Casserly
Grace E. King
Grace Gallatin
Grace Greenwood
Grant Allen
Guillermo A. Sherwell
Gulielma Zollinger
Gustav Flaubert
H. A. Cody
H. B. Irving
H.C. Bailey
H. G. Wells
H. H. Munro
H. Irving Hancock
H. R. Naylor
H. Rider Haggard
H. W. C. Davis
Haldeman Julius
Hall Caine
Hamilton Wright Mabie
Hans Christian Andersen
Harold Avery
Harold McGrath
Harriet Beecher Stowe
Harry Castlemon
Harry Coghill
Harry Houidini

Hayden Carruth
Helent Hunt Jackson
Helen Nicolay
Hendrik Conscience
Hendy David Thoreau
Henri Barbusse
Henrik Ibsen
Henry Adams
Henry Ford
Henry Frost
Henry James
Henry Jones Ford
Henry Seton Merriman
Henry W Longfellow
Herbert A. Giles
Herbert Carter
Herbert N. Casson
Herman Hesse
Hildegard G. Frey
Homer
Honore De Balzac
Horace B. Day
Horace Walpole
Horatio Alger Jr.
Howard Pyle
Howard R. Garis
Hugh Lofting
Hugh Walpole
Humphry Ward
Ian Maclaren
Inez Haynes Gillmore
Irving Bacheller
Isabel Cecilia Williams
Isabel Hornibrook
Israel Abrahams
Ivan Turgenev
J.G.Austin
J. Henri Fabre
J. M. Barrie
J. M. Walsh
J. Macdonald Oxley
J. R. Miller
J. S. Fletcher
J. S. Knowles
J. Storer Clouston
J. W. Duffield
Jack London
Jacob Abbott
James Allen
James Andrews
James Baldwin

James Branch Cabell
James DeMille
James Joyce
James Lane Allen
James Lane Allen
James Oliver Curwood
James Oppenheim
James Otis
James R. Driscoll
Jane Abbott
Jane Austen
Jane L. Stewart
Janet Aldridge
Jens Peter Jacobsen
Jerome K. Jerome
Jessie Graham Flower
John Buchan
John Burroughs
John Cournos
John F. Kennedy
John Gay
John Glasworthy
John Habberton
John Joy Bell
John Kendrick Bangs
John Milton
John Philip Sousa
John Taintor Foote
Jonas Lauritz Idemil Lie
Jonathan Swift
Joseph A. Altsheler
Joseph Carey
Joseph Conrad
Joseph E. Badger Jr
Joseph Hergesheimer
Joseph Jacobs
Jules Vernes
Julian Hawthrone
Julie A Lippmann
Justin Huntly McCarthy
Kakuzo Okakura
Karle Wilson Baker
Kate Chopin
Kenneth Grahame
Kenneth McGaffey
Kate Langley Bosher
Kate Langley Bosher
Katherine Cecil Thurston
Katherine Stokes
L. A. Abbot
L. T. Meade

L. Frank Baum
Latta Griswold
Laura Dent Crane
Laura Lee Hope
Laurence Housman
Lawrence Beasley
Leo Tolstoy
Leonid Andreyev
Lewis Carroll
Lewis Sperry Chafer
Lilian Bell
Lloyd Osbourne
Louis Hughes
Louis Joseph Vance
Louis Tracy
Louisa May Alcott
Lucy Fitch Perkins
Lucy Maud Montgomery
Luther Benson
Lydia Miller Middleton
Lyndon Orr
M. Corvus
M. H. Adams
Margaret E. Sangster
Margret Howth
Margaret Vandercook
Margaret W. Hungerford
Margret Penrose
Maria Edgeworth
Maria Thompson Daviess
Mariano Azuela
Marion Polk Angellotti
Mark Overton
Mark Twain
Mary Austin
Mary Catherine Crowley
Mary Cole
Mary Hastings Bradley
Mary Roberts Rinehart
Mary Rowlandson
M. Wollstonecraft Shelley
Maud Lindsay
Max Beerbohm
Myra Kelly
Nathaniel Hawthrone
Nicolo Machiavelli
O. F. Walton
Oscar Wilde

Owen Johnson
P.G. Wodehouse
Paul and Mabel Thorne
Paul G. Tomlinson
Paul Severing
Percy Brebner
Percy Keese Fitzhugh
Peter B. Kyne
Plato
Quincy Allen
R. Derby Holmes
R. L. Stevenson
R. S. Ball
Rabindranath Tagore
Rahul Alvares
Ralph Bonehill
Ralph Henry Barbour
Ralph Victor
Ralph Waldo Emmerson
Rene Descartes
Ray Cummings
Rex Beach
Rex E. Beach
Richard Harding Davis
Richard Jefferies
Richard Le Gallienne
Robert Barr
Robert Frost
Robert Gordon Anderson
Robert L. Drake
Robert Lansing
Robert Lynd
Robert Michael Ballantyne
Robert W. Chambers
Rosa Nouchette Carey
Rudyard Kipling
Saint Augustine
Samuel B. Allison
Samuel Hopkins Adams
Sarah Bernhardt
Sarah C. Hallowell
Selma Lagerlof
Sherwood Anderson
Sigmund Freud
Standish O'Grady
Stanley Weyman
Stella Benson
Stella M. Francis

Stephen Crane
Stewart Edward White
Stijn Streuvels
Swami Abhedananda
Swami Parmananda
T. S. Ackland
T. S. Arthur
The Princess Der Ling
Thomas A. Janvier
Thomas A Kempis
Thomas Anderton
Thomas Bailey Aldrich
Thomas Bulfinch
Thomas De Quincey
Thomas Dixon
Thomas H. Huxley
Thomas Hardy
Thomas More
Thornton W. Burgess
U. S. Grant
Upton Sinclair
Valentine Williams
Various Authors
Vaughan Kester
Victor Appleton
Victor G. Durham
Victoria Cross
Virginia Woolf
Wadsworth Camp
Walter Camp
Walter Scott
Washington Irving
Wilbur Lawton
Wilkie Collins
Willa Cather
Willard F. Baker
William Dean Howells
William le Queux
W. Makepeace Thackeray
William W. Walter
William Shakespeare
Winston Churchill
Yei Theodora Ozaki
Yogi Ramacharaka
Young E. Allison
Zane Grey